Jeff Jones

MAUREEN GIBBON

thief

Maureen Gibbon is the author of *Swimming Sweet Arrow*, a novel, and *Magdalena*, a collection of prose poems. A graduate of the Iowa Writers' Workshop, she has received a Bush Foundation Artist Fellowship, two Loft McKnight Artist Fellowships, and a residency at the Santa Fe Art Institute. She lives in northern Minnesota, where she teaches writing.

ALSO BY MAUREEN GIBBON

Swimming Sweet Arrow

Magdalena

thief

thief

MAUREEN GIBBON

SARAH CRICHTON BOOKS

FARRAR, STRAUS AND GIROUX   NEW YORK

SARAH CRICHTON BOOKS
Farrar, Straus and Giroux
18 West 18th Street, New York 10011

Printed in the United States of America
First edition, 2010

Library of Congress Cataloging-in-Publication Data
Gibbon, Maureen.
  Thief / Maureen Gibbon. — 1st ed.
    p.   cm.
  "Sarah Crichton books."
  ISBN 978-0-374-27454-2 (pbk. : alk. paper)
  1. Triangles (Interpersonal relations)—Fiction.   2. Minnesota—Fiction.
I. Title.

PS3557.I39167T47   2010
813'.54—dc22

2009042275

Designed by Abby Kagan

www.fsgbooks.com
P1

Things are always different from what they might be.

—HENRY JAMES, *The Portrait of a Lady*

thief

1

BEFORE I MET ALPHA BREVILLE, all I knew about Stillwater, Minnesota, was that antique shops and a cloying quaintness filled its downtown. I'd gone there once on a Prozac-induced spending spree and come home with an ink-stained quilt, a book of Jesse Stuart stories, and about thirty old photographs I'd stolen from various stores and shoved past my jeans into my underwear. The photographs were worthless, but Prozac made me compulsive, and I couldn't stop myself from falling in love with the old-time faces.

My favorite photo, the one I framed and hung on the wall beside my bed, was of a man who looked to be in his forties, and who struck me as being a country preacher. He wore a dark suit and limp string tie, his expression was patient and sorrowful, and in spite of careful slicking back, his hair sprouted cowlicks at his forehead and above each ear. Across the bottom of the dirty cream slip that held the photograph, someone had penciled *t-h-e-i-f*. It was partly that misspelled word that made me fall in love with the photo, and I wondered who had labeled the man: a family member who judged and banished, or the thief himself, giving himself penance by owning up to his misdoing. I decided it was the latter, but probably only because the photographer had tinted the cheeks of the man a faint red, and the color looked like hot shame.

I met Alpha Breville after he (along with a grave digger and an engineer) answered a personal ad I had placed in a weekly paper. When his letter came to me with his prison number as part of the return address, I thought it was laughable that a convict believed he had something to offer me in terms of dating, and I questioned how an inmate at Stillwater state prison even got the $2 the paper charged to forward responses. I thought about throwing away Breville's letter, but it was somehow impossible to do. Even with the return prison address, the airy white envelope held the promise that all letters held. So I read the thing, and after I did, it seemed the joke was on me, because the letter Alpha Breville wrote to me from Stillwater state prison was no different from the other letters I'd received in response to my ad. There was an explanation of why he had chosen to write (my headline "Great kisser, good listener" caught his eye), followed by a short personal history and accounting of years, a series of questions for me, and a conclusion expressing hope that I would write back. An ordinary letter. I don't know why that surprised me so much—after all, there is only so much that can go into a letter, and it was in Breville's best interests to make himself sound like any other man. But it was the ordinariness of his letter that startled me. If what a convict wrote was no different from what other men wrote, maybe he himself was not so different.

Yet something was different. In explaining that he came from a town in western South Dakota, Breville wrote that though he missed his family and the land, he did not miss living there with its isolation. It was a thoughtful observation and one that meant something to me, since I'd spent time in South Dakota and knew how it could feel. But the part of Breville's letter that really got my attention was the part that came next, his description of a sunset: *In the summer, the sun is the color of orangeade and fierce when it sets. You think it's going to stay burned in your eyes forever.*

It was just a couple of sentences—strings of words. But he was absolutely right. The summer I was out there, the sun really didn't look like anything natural on this earth, and if I watched it too long as it slowly set behind the flat line of the horizon, I would be blinded to all color for a long time after. Of all the things men had written in their letters—paragraphs about seeking "friendship" or "that special someone," or clever descriptions of what they liked to do in their spare time—nothing struck me more than Breville's words about the nuclear-looking South Dakota sun.

Of course, in that first letter Breville didn't tell me the most important detail: why he was in Stillwater. The omission itself seemed damning, but even as I thought that, I also understood his choice. Either his incarceration would repel me so much it wouldn't matter what he'd done, or else I would write back and, in doing so, give him an opportunity to explain. It was the only decision he could make, the only gamble he could take, and anyone smart enough to construct a very normal letter would be smart enough to take that chance. After all, I told myself, Rochester didn't come right out and tell Jane Eyre he had a crazy wife in the attic—he didn't tell until he had to.

The book was still on my mind because I'd finished the school year with it, teaching it to the seniors. When we got to the section where Bertha's presence at Thornfield was revealed, most students said they could understand Rochester's decision to conceal the truth. They believed almost to a person that Jane would never have even "given him a chance" if he'd revealed everything at the outset. When I pressed further, though, and asked them if they didn't think that such an omission was a type of lie, they uncomfortably agreed it was. *But still*, they'd said. *But still.*

In any case, I suppose it was partly because of *Jane Eyre* that I decided to take things one step further and write back to Breville. And it wasn't because I had some romantic notion that I was Jane and Breville was Rochester. It's just that thinking of *Jane Eyre* made me remember I had enough of my own secrets to know they couldn't be the first things told.

I'd always been interested in black sheep and underdogs. When I was a young girl, I liked boys with wolfish faces, who had a bit of the hoodlum in them, and my tastes still ran that way. My most recent relationship started when I saw a man get off a bus on Lake Street, and he saw me see him. We circled each other on Hennepin until he came up and began talking to me. I didn't care that he worked as a dishwasher. I liked his face and his body, and I was glad that he liked mine. Even in my job, where I played the role of maiden aunt, I often went out of my way to help delinquent boys and wayward girls. I saw in those students pieces of myself, but more importantly I tried to see them *as they were*, with dignity. I believed each of them had a voice and a story, and at least some of them reflected that belief back to me. For instance, last year Danielle Starck wrote on the back of her school picture, *Your class was the reason I came to school.* The following semester, when she wasn't my student, she tried to kill herself. I'm not saying I could have stopped her—I was only an English teacher—but maybe I could have helped her. I do know I would have tried.

It was that kind of thinking, in part, that made me give Alpha Breville a chance.

2

THOUGH I WAS INDICATING MY OPENNESS by the very act of writing back to Breville, I thought it would be best if I sounded guarded in my reply. So after my greeting to him, I wrote, "I'm not sure why you answered my ad. I'm looking for someone to date, and you can't offer me that. Frankly, I don't know what you can offer anyone. But perhaps we can exchange a few letters. You seem like a thoughtful enough person."

Even that slight compliment seemed like a risk, however, so I followed it up immediately. "While I understand why you might be reluctant to tell me why you're in Stillwater, you must know you have to," I wrote. "I expect complete honesty. Surely you can see the need for it. I have to know how you came to be in prison. If you can't tell me that, I would prefer you didn't write back at all."

I didn't bother to say that I could find out anything about him I wanted—it was true, even in those days before the Internet. Whatever Breville had done was a matter of public record, and I was sure he knew it. Then I sent off my letter, an ink-jetted copy as depersonalized as I could make it. If he wanted to respond to my question, he could, and if he didn't, I stood nothing to lose.

When I didn't hear back for a week, when no plain white envelope with the Stillwater return address showed up in my mailbox, I figured my price—honesty—had been too high for Breville to pay. And I thought it was for the best. Whatever the reason was for Breville's incarceration, I didn't need the drama. I'd come up north to a rented lake cabin the day school let out, and in the days after I sent my letter to Stillwater, I did all the things I'd driven four hours north to do: I swam, I went for walks around the lake, and I watched birds—loons and eagles, and a great blue heron that crossed so low over the water I could hear its wing-beats. In the afternoons, after the worst of the sun's burning was over, I took a small pillow down to the dock and slept on the hard boards. I never thought I would be able to sleep in the light and sound and breeze of the day, but I always did. And when I woke—groggy and hot—I'd climb down off the dock and slip into the deliciously cold water. It amazed me that I felt so at ease in a place I'd never been before. Part of me wanted to tell someone about how the days felt, but another part of me wanted to keep it secret. Mostly I just wanted to go on feeling the way I did.

The lack of response from Breville gave me time to think, and I began to believe that my willingness to write to him was just another sign of being adrift. While my work life was stable and pleasant enough, pieces of my personal life were in their usual disarray, and I was glad I hadn't told any of my friends about writing to Breville, since I knew what their reactions would be. My friend Kate would rush on to another subject, trying to be nonjudgmental yet judging all the time, and Julian would castigate me. He knew everything that had gone on this past year, and why I'd decided to move out of my apartment and put some space between me and my old life in the Cities. "What is wrong with you?" I could hear him asking. "You just got rid of one dangerous asshole. Do you need to invite another into your life?"

To a certain degree he would be right—I did love danger. Adventure. There was a part of me that was content being an English teacher, living in book-lined rooms, writing poetry, hanging out with friends. But sometimes those things didn't satisfy me, and like most people, I led a double life—and at times even a triple life. I was one person during the week, another with friends, and someone entirely different on weekends when I went out. I said I wanted a healthy relationship with a man, but I did nothing to find one. Instead, I patched together half-relationships and weekly assignations. I did nothing to unite the disparate pieces of my life. But as I always pointed out to Julian, I didn't want to marry any of the men I dated—I only wanted to kiss them and fuck them. I knew how to draw the line. I also knew writing back to Breville had probably been foolish, and I knew it without any loving, meddlesome friend pointing it out to me.

And then a letter came. And I could tell by the heft of it that Breville had decided to tell me his story.

I didn't open the letter the way I often opened my mail, right there at the mailbox, or walking the gravel road back to the cabin— I waited until I got inside. I don't know why. Maybe I didn't want to read in the bright June sunlight that Breville was a drug dealer, a thief, or convicted of some kind of assault, or maybe I already felt too secretive about the correspondence to begin reading on the public road. All I know is that as I opened the envelope, I tried to ready myself for what I might find. Yet when I started thinking that burglary would be a more acceptable crime than, say, assault, the idea of preparation seemed silly. Whatever Breville had done, it had been serious enough to land him in Stillwater, and no amount of rationalizing on my part would change that.

Breville began by thanking me for the opportunity to tell me about himself and then apologized for taking so long to reply to my request. *It took me a while to write back because I don't like to think about the details of my crime*, he wrote. *But, yes, you are right, you have the right to know.*

At nineteen, Breville said, he was a thief and a drinker, "a user and an abuser." He took any drug he could get his hands on, though he preferred alcohol and marijuana because they were the easiest to get. His only idea of a good time, he said, was when he could get wasted. One night when he had been out drinking and partying with friends, he decided to break into a house in South Minneapolis because he wanted more money.

> I was only going to steal what I saw through the window. A TV and a stereo. I didn't think anyone was at home. But when I got inside the house, the woman who lived there heard me. She came out into the living room to investigate. I didn't see or hear her at first but then she asked me what I was doing. She was wearing just a robe and I saw part of her breast. That's when I decided to rape her. I didn't plan to do it but, I did it.

Breville went on to say that he believed he would not have raped the woman if he hadn't been drinking that night, but he said he also realized that was no excuse:

> I was a different person when I was drinking. Crazy. But that was also part of my crime, or at least part of my sickness. I have been sober for seven years, in a 12-step program. But I doubt I would have changed at all if I hadn't been sent to prison. I'd be out there running the streets. Or maybe I'd be dead. I don't know.

Breville told me he received more than the mandatory sentence because he pled innocent to the rape and showed no remorse. Even though police found some of the woman's possessions in his apartment the morning after the rape, he thought he could beat the charge because his lawyer told him there was no DNA evidence.

> I was in denial then about my crime. But I did it. I raped that woman. That is my crime. If you do not want to write me again I will understand. I will more than understand.

After I finished reading Breville's letter, I let the pages drop to the floor. I didn't do it to seem dramatic—there was no one there to see the gesture. I dropped the pages because I didn't want to hold them anymore. Breville had sat in his cell writing the letter—for days, if what he told me was truthful—and now the pages were here in the kitchen of the cabin, and I didn't want to touch them. I didn't want that proximity to Breville. I didn't even want to see his handwriting on the cheap notebook paper.

The letter stayed on the floor for days. I walked past it at first, and then I pushed it under the kitchen table with my foot. I told myself not to think about it, but I did think about it. I thought about it when I was swimming, and when I lay on the dock, reading or writing in my journal. I thought about it when I talked in the yard with Merle, the old man who was renting me the cabin for the summer, and I thought about it as I drank my morning coffee under the birch tree. And what I thought was that the whole thing was a colossal joke, some ridiculous trick the universe was intent on playing on me. I place a personal ad in a paper and a rapist responds. But in a while, that idea passed, too, if only because I knew the universe wasn't particular enough to single me out. In one way, what had happened was an ugly sort of coincidence, but in another way, it was predictable enough. One lonely person placed an ad, and another lonely person had answered, and who else could be lonelier than a rapist in Stillwater state prison?

Days after receiving Breville's letter, I picked it up and read it again. Not because of some sick impulse, as Julian would say, but because I thought maybe the letter represented a different kind of chance—an opportunity, if you will. I picked the letter off the floor because I thought maybe Alpha Breville and I had something to say to each other. I had been raped when I was sixteen, and he had raped when he was nineteen.

We were two sides of a coin.

3

ONCE I DECIDED that Breville and I might have something to say to each other, I could not stop thinking about the idea. If he could tell me why he had raped, maybe I could somehow make sense of the one ejaculation that so transfigured my life. His crime became the very reason to write back to him. Yet I knew the letter I wrote would not be the one he hoped to receive.

"You must be the unluckiest of people to have chosen my ad to respond to," I began. "I was raped when I was sixteen years old, one week before I turned seventeen." Then I told him some of the details of my rape and how it had affected me.

I never dated blond men, because my rapist was blond. I couldn't stand certain smells, because my rapist's hair and breath had been foul. I had a hard time sleeping beside a man, even if I was in an intimate relationship with him, because I could not let myself relax. I never entirely lost the feeling of dirtiness and infection, perhaps because I had, in fact, been infected with gonorrhea and herpes. I described in detail for him the ulcers and scarring and how, in some fluke, I had spread the virus to one of my eyes and almost lost vision there. I told Breville I still carried a sense of shame about the whole thing, even though it had happened seventeen years ago.

"I cannot say my life was derailed by what happened," I wrote. "I think I have had success in spite of it. But I think about the experience almost every single day, and I sometimes wonder who I might have been if it hadn't happened. I would guess you had a similar devastating effect on the woman you raped. She probably tries to pretend you don't exist—you are not even a person to her. But when she does think of you, I'm sure she hates you as much as I hate the man who raped me. To me, he is a useless piece of shit littering the earth."

I wrote the letter in a fever of remembering and anger, and when I sent it off, I suppose there was some kind of catharsis. But mostly I just felt upset by the old memories and overwhelmed by emotions. Still, I thought it was good that I had written the letter, and that some of my anger had come out. It had been freeing to say some of the ugly things I wanted to say. I said to Breville what I hadn't been able to say to my rapist. My rapist—what a phrase. I mean the man who raped me, he of the festering cock.

As days went by and I received no response, I became sure Breville would not write back. I couldn't blame him. Even if he were the loneliest person in all of Stillwater state prison, I couldn't imagine anyone welcoming that kind of rage into his life, and I was nothing if not filled with rage. Sometimes friends saw small flickers of anger and impatience in me, but almost no one knew about the uncontrollable fits I sometimes had. Sometimes I beat my bed with hangers or broke dishes or phones. From the outside, my actions might have appeared comical, but the feelings behind the outbursts weren't. However, most of the time my anger didn't translate into any action at all. When I didn't live up to my own standards, when I mishandled a decision, or even when something happened over which I had little or no control, I turned my anger inward, against myself. Even when I thought I'd come to the end of it, after I'd gained some crucial insight or felt peaceful for a long time, something would happen and my fury would return. Circle back into my life.

That destruction and depression was part of what I wanted to work out. If I had an audience—not friends or a therapist but someone real and deserving of anger—maybe it would make a difference. Maybe the thing that was inside me would finally find a different and worthy target. Breville was not my rapist, but he was someone's rapist. Not mine but someone's.

When Breville wrote back a week later, he told me it had been hard to read my letter, and that he had stopped a few times and put it away. But he also said he felt obligated to read what I wrote, believing it was part of his fate:

> By listening to you, I learn how my crime probably affected the woman I hurt. I thought I understood before but, reading your letter I see I didn't. It's not that I didn't know what I did was serious but I didn't understand the half of it. I didn't understand the anger she must feel or maybe I didn't want to understand. Suzanne, if I can somehow make things up to you or be of some use to you, then I will be doing something.

When I first read that, I felt a kind of righteousness, but the feeling quickly changed. I didn't believe Breville understood how a cock could be like a knife, or how quickly and carelessly and violently he had changed a woman's life. I didn't think he could understand—he was the perpetrator and the penetrator. I began to wonder if his letter wasn't all just bullshit, the result of learning the right things to say in his prison 12-step program.

I thought of not responding, but it seemed like my duty to

confront him. Even the confiding way he'd used my name in the middle of the letter—as if we were friends or intimates—bothered me. I wanted to repel and ridicule him, so I began my reply with no salutation, just his name and a comma. "This is a piece of paper," I wrote. "How stupid to think anything you read or write in a letter can make up for what you did to that woman in South Minneapolis. I suppose you are a step ahead of the man who raped me because you at least are serving time for your crime, but there is no way to bring the score back to nil. You can't do anything for me or with me to make up for your crime. Nothing. There is no trading on sorrow."

It again took Breville several days to respond, but he did reply. In this letter, he told me he understood he could never erase the past or his crime.

But if I dwell only on that it means I can't ever change anything. You may not believe this because you don't know me but I have changed from the person I was when I raped. I've had choices to make in here about how I serve my time and I've tried to make good ones. I work as much as they permit me. I take college classes and one day I hope I can work with troubled kids, the kind I was. I'm clean and sober. I know you are saying what choice do I have? But I do have a choice. You can get drugs in here if you want. I choose not to. I can't change the past but I am working to change the future. I do not want to live the way I lived before. Even if your letters are harsh to read they are good for me, I know. I do not ever want to be in denial again about what I did. I think I have caused you enough pain by making you think about a terrible time in your life and I would understand if you didn't want to write back. But if you choose to write to me again, I will be grateful. I know I have nothing to offer you, except maybe to give you someone to hate.

I didn't know what to believe when I finished Breville's letter—
I didn't know what to think anymore. I put the handwritten pages
down on the kitchen table and walked outside, into the sunlight
and down to the water.

But even as I swam, I kept thinking about Breville's last
phrase—*to give you someone to hate.* It seemed like a self-immolating
thing to offer, and impossible, but it made me think of how seldom
anyone offered me anything. I didn't mean friends—Julian loved
me, and so did Kate, and I felt their love and friendship in real and
tangible ways. But men? Even when one offered me something, I
knew he wanted something in return. And yet Breville seemed to
be offering something for nothing, and something I needed, because even when I did understand where my anger came from, the
understanding still didn't give me any control over it. Maybe I did
need someone to hate.

If it turned out Breville was lying, that he did want something
in return, I would be free to walk away. To continue or not. He
couldn't show up at my house or job, he couldn't call me—I held all
the cards. I was free to work out whatever I could on him. And that
was what I wanted: to take out on Breville what I couldn't take out
on my rapist and what I had been taking out on myself all these
years.

I wanted to use Breville.

4

INSTEAD OF WITHDRAWING as Breville thought I would, I told him I would continue to write to him as long as I felt able. "I feel like I still have questions to ask you. But when I decide to stop writing, you'll have to accept it," I wrote. "I owe you no explanation."

Perhaps it was ridiculous to insist I was in control—after all, Breville was locked up in a maximum-security prison. But the ability to stop things was essential for me. There certainly had been times a man called it off with me, but when I was the one to end a relationship, I always did it in a complete way, breaking off all contact. When I broke the lease on my apartment and came up north, Richaux, my ex, had no way of finding me. He would have created every possible scene if I had let him, and by leaving as I did, I'd avoided all of that. Julian was convinced I had an addiction to dangerous men, and I could not deny it, but I did not let any man work out his inflated notion of himself on me. If I sometimes had to uproot myself and begin again, at a deficit, then I did. Contrary to what Julian thought, the line I would not cross did exist. So if I chose to go on writing to Breville, it was exactly that: my choice. I did not do anything I didn't want to do.

In the same letter in which I told Breville he would have to accept my terms, I asked him a question about his description of the rape he'd committed. A couple of sentences in particular disturbed me. It was odd, perhaps, to focus on a couple of sentences when everything he wrote was so disturbing, but there was one detail of his crime I felt I had to understand.

I wrote, "You told me that when you got inside the house in South Minneapolis, when you watched the woman come into the room and 'saw part of her breast'—that that's when you 'decided to rape her.' Yet how can that be? If you had been a different kind of person, you would never have made that decision. Don't you see? The decision was in you for longer than that moment. It was part of you. Maybe it only came out that night in South Minneapolis, but it would never have been able to come out if it hadn't been somewhere inside you already. It was part of who you were. It's like what people do when they are drinking and say something awful, and then they claim, 'Oh, that was the alcohol talking.' They pretend it wasn't really them. But it is them. It is perhaps the truest representation of what is inside them. Just as your actions that night in South Minneapolis were a true representation of you. How could you have made the decision to rape in an instant? That violence was inside you then, and, I believe, is still part of you today."

After I wrote that, though, I wondered about the truthfulness of it. Part of me believed people revealed their true selves when they drank because so many of their inhibitions dropped away. I knew it was true for me: nothing I did or said when I was drinking surprised me. The crudeness of my behavior might embarrass me, but I knew it was my own personality asserting itself. Yet the opposite was also true. How many times had I drunkenly spent the night with a man, fucking him with enthusiasm and desire—only to be grateful to see the door close on him the next day when I was sober? The fuck and the intimacy had been genuine, but so were my daytime thoughts of retreat. Sometimes my desire for solitude was so strong I couldn't even last a night with a man. If I was the one staying over, I might leave in the early morning hours, stealthily, or after making some excuse about why I had to get home.

In fact, the contrast between daytime and nighttime thoughts was what prevented me from taking half relationships and weekly assignations seriously. What I wanted at night was sometimes entirely unrelated to what I was willing to contend with day to day. And I knew other people must feel the same. If they didn't, Etta James wouldn't sing about wanting a "Sunday Kind of Love." So maybe I was wrong about Breville. Maybe he wouldn't have committed the rape if he hadn't been drinking.

I walked outside then. To clear my head and to get away from the circle my thoughts had made.

Earlier in the morning it had rained, hard, and the gravel road still showed pocks and ribbons. I'd only walked a little way when I saw something crossing ahead of me, small and low to the ground. When I got to the place, I looked in the grass and saw a salamander. Not much bigger than a finger, it stood still long enough for me to study it—a dark, moist thing with tiny spots and beads for eyes—and then it disappeared into the tall weeds. I walked all the way to the north end of the lake after that. At first I was thinking about Breville, but in a while I wasn't. In a while it was just me out on a cool morning walk.

When I got back to the cabin, I printed out my letter as it was and signed it. I didn't use any closing, just my name, the only thing to appear in cursive. *Suzanne.* The walk had made things plain again. It was one thing if drinking made you want to screw a good-looking and willing stranger, and quite another if it made you break into a woman's house and rape her. And so I reminded myself that Breville was the criminal, not me.

5

A FEW DAYS LATER when I went to pick up my mail, I saw Merle
standing by the mailbox at the end of his drive. The cabin I was
renting was on a portion of his land and had no separate street address, so I shared Merle's mailbox. A couple of times he walked
down to the cabin with mail for me, but since I'd been writing to
Breville, I'd been trying to beat him to it. Not today, though—
today I'd been in the water, and the water was so cool and pleasant
I'd just gone on swimming and swimming.

"I believe it's all for you," Merle said. "I only got the paper."

He handed me the pile of envelopes with Breville's letter on
top. I didn't know if Merle had seen the return address or not, or if
he'd been able to decipher what a letter with a Stillwater address
and long number meant—and I didn't know that I cared. Still, I
turned the pile of mail in my hand so the address was facing
down.

"You must be quite a swimmer to stay out as long as you do."

"I don't swim very fast."

"Still. Most people around here don't swim. Just kids. Adults
lose the knack of it."

"Do you swim?"

"I did until a few years ago," Merle said. "Now I just feel the cold."

If he'd been younger, perhaps I would have felt odd standing there and talking in my bathing suit, my towel wrapped around my waist, my hair streeling down my shoulders. I could feel him watching me, taking me in, but I didn't feel funny about it. He was my father's age and he seemed to treat me carefully, with some sort of distance or respect—I couldn't quite tell which. In any case, I didn't feel uncomfortable or exposed standing there with him, and I saw as clearly as I saw the lake in front of me that he wanted to go on talking to me in the sunshine.

"Do you miss it?" I said. "Swimming?"

"I miss it. But I miss a number of things," he said. "And I still enjoy watching the lake as much as I ever did. Did you hear the wolves the other night?"

"Was that what it was? I thought maybe they were coyotes."

"We have those, too. But no, that was a wolf pack. You hear them only once in a while."

"Well, I did hear them," I said. "They woke me up."

"I was awake already. It's a grand sound."

"It was. That's a good word for it."

"Well, enjoy the lake and the day," he said then, turning to go, as if he knew he was keeping me. "It's a pleasure to see someone swimming."

"It's a pleasure to be here. Thanks for renting the cabin to me."

He waved his hand. "You're paying me. I'm the one should be thanking you."

But the truth was he was hardly making any money off me. If he wanted, he could have rented the place for much more than what he was charging me because that's how it was in summer—resorts charged $1,000 a week for rustic cabins. But I figured Merle wouldn't have rented to just anyone. I'd gotten the cabin by placing an ad in the local paper in which I tried to make myself sound responsible and appealing: *Quiet schoolteacher seeks small cabin to rent for summer. References available.*

"It isn't much of a place," Merle told me somewhat gruffly when I called him on the phone. "It was never meant to be fancy."

Yet after just a few minutes of talking, he invited me up to take a look around, and in another couple of minutes he said, "Well, if you find you like it, it's yours. What would you think of five hundred dollars?"

I hadn't thought things would move so quickly, so I was taken off guard. "I know it's a more than fair price," I said. "But I can't afford that much a week."

"No, I meant five hundred a month. I don't want to be greedy."

That's how we sealed the deal. The sense I got from talking to him on the phone was quickly confirmed when I met him. He was renting to me because he wanted another person around. Not company—he was too private for that—but a presence. Someone to watch from the window or see out by the mailbox.

It was a tenuous and temporary role—the kind of relationship I felt comfortable in. And if part of it meant standing and talking once in a while in the sunshine, in my bathing suit, I didn't care.

I took Breville's letter down to the dock to read. I could have read it in the privacy of the cabin, but this day I didn't want that. I wanted to read it out in the sun, with my feet dangling in the cool water. I didn't know why, but it seemed to matter at that moment to have everything out in the open. Maybe I felt stronger that way. *I'm not sure I can explain any better than I have how that night happened, and not because I don't want to*, Breville wrote.

I would do anything I could for you. But I've gone over and over it in my mind, and the best way I can describe it is to say that when I saw that woman, I made the decision to rape her. In some ways my actions are still a mystery to me. But if you're asking if I ever had dreams or fantasies before that night of raping a woman, I can say no I did not. But nothing about that night is crystal clear to me. I was drunk and high and not in my right mind. All I know for certain is that I remember seeing her standing there in a bath-robe, and I saw part of her breast, and the decision was made. It's almost like my body made it. But if I could do anything to take it back, I would. And maybe it's like you say, the decision was in me all along. I know I was a hell-raiser and always getting into fights, so yes, I had violence in me. I will admit sometimes I feel like I don't know how to take responsibility for my actions because I don't even know the person I was that night. But, it doesn't mat-ter. I was the one who committed the crime. And I accept your terms for friendship. Or maybe we are not friends, maybe it is the wishful part of me saying that. But, whether or not I am your friend, you can count on me to be yours, even if I never hear from you again.

I read Breville's letter through a few times sitting down there on the dock, and then I tucked the thing under my towel so it wouldn't blow away. Yet even after I lay down on the hard boards and pillowed my head on my arms and drifted in and out of sleep, I kept thinking about Breville's words. It wasn't lost on me that, in Breville's position, any letter, even one filled with anger and in-sults, might be a welcome variation in the day. In that sense, as long as I kept on writing, I was giving him something he wanted. But it seemed to me my letters were serving as some kind of penance. Breville took whatever I wrote to him—took it and told me it was good for him—and that somehow disarmed me.

Maybe it was the combination of that thought and being down by the water, daydreaming and sleeping in the sun, but after a while I began to feel a kind of forgiveness. I don't mean that I forgave Breville for raping the woman in South Minneapolis, or that I forgave Frank L— for raping me.

What I mean is I began to forgive myself for being raped all those years ago.

By reading Breville's account of the rape, I'd come to understand something about why I'd been raped at sixteen. In his letter Breville said he had intended only to steal, but when he saw the woman standing there, he decided, just like that, to rape her. He claimed he never would have done it if he hadn't been drinking, but whatever the rationalization, it was clear his decision to rape had nothing whatever to do with the woman. When I realized that, I understood for the first time that my own rape had nothing to do with me. I had been the random focus of someone else's decision, but the decision had nothing to do with me.

Which is to say: I was raped for no reason.

6

I USUALLY CALLED JULIAN in the early evening—after he had time to slough off the day but before he headed out to a movie or for drinks with friends. Sometimes he ate his dinner while I talked to him, since he told me that was what he missed most about me: the two of us sharing a swordfish dinner on the terrace of our favorite Greek restaurant.

This night as he ate, I wanted to tell him what was going on with Breville, but somehow I couldn't bring myself to do it. Instead I told him how I'd been sitting on the dock that afternoon, dangling my feet in the water, when I felt a tiny tap on the bottom of my foot. It was so gentle it didn't startle me, and when I looked down, I saw a painted turtle lazily swimming and floating through the water.

"I think he was napping," I said. "I think he just drifted into my foot."

"Aren't there any groups you can join up there?" Julian said. "Any people you can meet?"

"I don't want to join a group. What do you mean?"

"The only person you talk to is that old man. Aren't there any Greens you can get to know? Some nice bleeding heart liberals?"

"So funny. I bet you could go onstage with that humor," I said. "Do I sound lonely?"

"I think you're getting isolated."

"That was the plan," I said. "I'm an introvert. If I don't have to make small talk with people until I'm back in the teachers' lounge, it will be fine with me."

I could hear Julian's fork go down on his plate, and, in a little while, a match striking and then an inhale. It made me miss him.

"Okay," he said, exhaling. "Maybe I'm wrong. But I think you need to connect with some people."

"All right."

"Go out to lunch with somebody."

"All right already," I said. "I know you're right."

But when I hung up the phone, I doubted I would do any of it. Maybe I was isolated, but I was also tired of people—I always was when the school year ended. Right now I was more interested in the herons and the felty way their wings sounded, or how, on some mornings, I made myself walk the gravel road around the lake until I found a feather on the ground. It never took long, and I always seemed to know just where to look.

That was what I had to talk about, or maybe it was all I wanted to talk about. I wasn't ready to tell Julian about Breville, not when it still felt too hard to explain to myself.

Even though Breville showed me my rape happened for no reason, I think it was inevitable that it did happen. Given who I was, even from an early age, it was probably inevitable some harm should come to me.

Though I was just sixteen when Frank L—— raped me, I was not a virgin or even virginal. At twelve I fooled around with boys in the woods, and by the time I was thirteen I already knew what counted was the size of my breasts and my skill at giving a hand job. While I liked school and had been praised by my teachers for the books I read and the poems I wrote, I quickly realized those activities were nearly useless.

I'm not sure how my perceptions started, but I assume it began with my own parents. There was the derisive, ugly way my father spoke to my mother in everyday conversation ("Dry up, old lady. Shut up and dry up . . ."); the lack of interest he showed in anything relating to her or my brother or me when measured against a drinking bout with his cronies; the pile of old *Playboy* and *Penthouse* magazines he had stacked in his closet, which I pored over whenever I was alone in the house. I liked looking at the women's breasts and vulvas, and was excited by them, though I doubt I could have explained my excitement at age nine or ten.

Yet it wasn't just my father. When I was fifteen and had a boyfriend in the army, I asked my mother to take pictures of me posing in my bathing suit so I could have something to send to Dale, and my mother consented. And though my one-piece bathing suit was modest enough, it was still a bathing suit, and it was still my mother taking the pictures. When the photos came back, I saw that in most of them, my mother had cut me off at the calf and top of the head, seemingly focusing the camera on my torso. The roll of film included a couple of full-length poses that showed all of me, and I picked those to send to Dale. The other photos, the chopped-off ones, were imperfect. Ruined. Still, I kept them, and now whenever I happened to come across the envelope in among other keepsakes, I marveled not only at my long, pretty legs, but also at the fact that a mother would take such photos of her fifteen-year-old daughter to send to a man.

But even those experiences did not explain who I was. There was a certain wildness in me that had nothing to do with my parents. It was solely mine, and had been since I was young. In the second and third grades, I played with other little girls in my neighborhood, and with one girl in particular. Our games always seemed to involve taking off our clothes and sucking on each other's nipples. When Shelagh stayed over one night, we spent an hour doing our familiar routine, and then Shelagh pulled away from my chest.

"This is getting kind of boring," she said. "What else can we do?"

I thought for a moment and then I said, "We can kiss each other there, where we pee."

"Won't it taste sour?"

I didn't know how to answer, so we didn't do it. Not long after, Shelagh moved away and I didn't see her again.

By fifth grade, I liked the shivery feeling I got whenever I heard one song that was always playing on the radio. *Sundown*, the song said, *you better take care.* The first time or two I heard the song I thought it was about a killing, a murder that took place in some frightening way. But then I listened to all the words and realized the song was about love. Love that made you creep around someone's back stairs. And even though I didn't understand anything about the adult side of the song—how love could be a dark thing, or how love could leave a person feeling angry and mean—because of the singer's voice I came to believe love could make you sullen and lost and dangerous. Like you were losing. I believed in the ideas even though I didn't fully understand them. Whatever the ideas meant, I knew I wanted to be like the woman in the song. Hard. Eleven years old, and that was what I wanted for myself, to have someone feel about me the way the man who sang the song felt about someone.

When I was fifteen, my twenty-two-year-old GI boyfriend had initiated me into all variations of intercourse before he went into Basic Training, and by sixteen I was so certain of the thing between my legs that I would let nothing else guide me. To have such sureness at that age is often perilous for young women, leading as it does to misalliances and children born too early. That was what my mother feared—but she needn't have. All I had to do was look at her life to know there was no connection between pleasure and children. I was not about to jeopardize my future or my pleasure by getting pregnant, and since I didn't want to mess around with pulling out or rubbers or all that stupidity, I went on birth control pills. I stayed on them through my teens and into my twenties and thirties.

So even if I was sixteen when Frank L—— raped me, I was a different sort of sixteen: not a virgin, in love with my own orgasms, already certain my main worth in the world was sexual. I don't mean I was aware that I thought of myself that way—I just thought I saw things as they were. That's what I mean when I say it was probably inevitable some harm should come to me. At sixteen I so much wanted to be part of the adult world, I started pounding on the door. Not surprisingly, it let me in.

7

I USUALLY SWAM FIRST THING, before too many people were out on the lake and before the sun shone high and hot. Sometimes I did a shallow dive off the end of the dock and plunged into the water, but this morning I felt quiet and slow, so I walked along the shoreline a little way, getting used to the water. When I walked past one jack pine that leaned out over the lake, though, I saw something that made me stop before I was even knee-deep.

A black shape was moving through the water. There in the shallows, the shape rose and turned, circled, turned again. Edges altered, and the thing kept shifting, rippling. It took me a few seconds to understand that the one shape was actually hundreds of shapes.

Each was ink-black, each one had horns and whiskers, and each swam above and beside and below its brothers and sisters. I looked around and saw the two parents swimming nearby, keeping watch. They were as big as my foot—or, put another way, as small as my foot.

I backed away. I backed away, but I kept watching the school of catfish and the black parents. The whole thing was so unexpected—

the fish were so dark and sinuous that I felt like I was watching some private rite. And as I backed away, the only thing I could think of besides the dark swirl was how I could describe it. Not to Kate, whom I hadn't seen since school had let out and to whom I'd sent one hastily written postcard, and not to Julian, and not just because of our last conversation.

I wanted to describe what I'd seen to Breville.

Our first letters back and forth had been so hard, filled with ugly details from my own rape and his crime, but that morning, by wanting to tell Breville about the sinuous school of baby catfish, I understood it was more than just me processing emotions from the rape from so many years ago. Maybe it was because I was away from friends, but by the time I actually wrote Breville a letter, I had been talking to him in my head for hours. I realized what he had predicted had somehow become true. He had become some type of friend to me.

It sounds like you saw a school of bullheads swimming, Breville wrote after he received my letter.

Black ones, from the sound of it, though there are also yellow and brown ones. You can bag as many as you like and they make good eating. I used to catch them sometimes at my grandpa's and they always put up a fight. But the way you describe them, they sound beautiful and I'm not sure I would ever want to catch one again. They want to live their bullhead lives too, don't they?

"I swam clear across the lake this evening," I wrote next. "I don't know how far it is, but it took me just about an hour of slow swimming to go from my dock to across the way and then back again. Merle said I could have asked him to follow me in a boat, but that would have ruined it, to have someone there. The maps say the lake goes 80 feet down in one spot, and I swam over it. Just me in my pink-flowered bathing suit."

Breville replied:

You don't know how I envy you. I haven't been swimming for the last seven years. Of course I haven't. The thing I remember about swimming in a lake is that you think the water will be colored somehow but it isn't. It is crystal clear when you look up at the sky. It would be good to feel what it's like to float again. Hell, I'd like to get water up my nose again. Ha ha. I would even be happy to shovel some snow these days. Though I guess that isn't likely in July, even in Minnesota. But seriously, the way you describe the lake I almost can feel it. How big is that lake anyway? It must be not too big if it took you half an hour to cross it, but it must not be too small either.

After reading Breville's letter, I thought if I could get a response written that day, and if I drove into town to mail it off, I might get a second letter back that week, on Saturday.

But almost as soon as I thought that, it seemed crazy. The idea that I had nothing better to do with my day than to write a letter, that I would make a special trip into town to mail it—all of it seemed foolish. Breville was a perfect correspondent because he was incarcerated. A convicted rapist with time on his hands. I was as isolated as Julian said I was. So I laid Breville's pages on the table. Left the cabin before I could change my mind and begin a reply.

Even though it was only nine o'clock at night, downtown was deserted except for the high school kids who took over the lower end of Main with their cars and music. I'd spent the day out, wading across the headwaters of the Mississippi at the state park and scouring antique shops for old photos. Just now I'd thoroughly poked around the small bookstore in town, accompanied by the resident beagle, who followed me from shelf to shelf until the store closed. But now all the touristy stores were closed and so was the Antler, where I could have at least gotten a cup of coffee. So I thought I'd have one drink and shoot the breeze with the bartender, and that would mark the end of the day of being out and about.

But it was not the bartender who was eager to talk to me at the Royal, the big bar on Main. Just moments after I got served, a guy came over and stood beside my barstool.

"Do you want to hear my new saying?" he asked me.

He looked to be in his forties, and he had both stringy hair and a receding hairline. He was also wearing a T-shirt that said MY BALLS ITCH.

"Well, I'll tell it to you anyway," he said. "'Shit happens. Flush it.' Pretty good, huh?"

I shook my head and said nothing.

"Can I buy you a beer?"

"I have a drink," I said.

"After you finish that."

"I'm not much of a drinker," I said, and slid down off the barstool. I was already thinking it had been a mistake to come in, but I figured there had to be at least one person in the place who had a better sense of fashion and free speech.

At the back of the bar there were pool tables and a jukebox, so I made my way there. As I checked out the music, I felt like I had drifted back in time as well as space because all the music was old rock about dirty deeds. The theme of the place became even more vivid to me when, in the short time I was standing there, the song changed from "Fat-Bottomed Girls" to "Big Balls."

"What're you going to play?"

It was the guy from the bar.

"Here's a quarter," he said. "You pick."

I was about to tell him I didn't need his hard-earned money, but before I could say anything, one of the pool players walked over, lightly holding his cue. He looked at me, and though my expression didn't change, I nodded slightly, acknowledging him. He looked down to rest the bottom of his cue on his boot, and then he looked at the guy from the bar.

"Leave her alone, buddy," he said.

My Balls Itch put up one hand. For a second it looked as if he might say something, but the wheels in his head turned and he thought better of it. Instead of talking, he just shook his head and walked away.

"He's a fuckhead," the player said. "He won't bother you no more."

"Thanks."

"You from around here?"

Even with his baseball cap on, I could see he had that close-cropped hair that young men favored. He was long and lanky, and his neck and face were burned red from the sun. His white T-shirt didn't say anything but it was gray around the collar.

"I'm up from the Cities," I said.

"This place is full of fuckheads. I'm less of a fuckhead than the rest, though."

"I see," I said. "Well, thanks again."

I put my drink down on a table and this time I kept walking to the very back of the bar, to the door with the exit sign above it and that I figured led onto the alley behind Main.

When I got outside there was still a bit of light in the sky. It looked electric blue and violet.

I knew there was some humor to it all. A restaurant in town advertised itself as "not a half-bad place to eat," and now I'd met someone who was less of a fuckhead than the rest. The town was nothing if not modest. I'd have to tell Julian about it.

He hadn't been wrong about my isolation, only about my willingness to do something about it. I wasn't a joiner, and maybe that was where I went wrong. If I'd ever taken the time to be part of something, I might have met a man with whom I had something in common. I might have at least stayed away from places like the Royal. But instead I was a loner. As much as I sometimes longed for company, I was like most loners—content with my discontent and happiest in my own company.

Somehow it was all easier to bear in that little town, though, under the blue-black sky. I got into my car and drove back home to the cabin.

8

THOUGH I TYPED my initial letters to Breville, I now usually hand-wrote them, keeping his most recent letter fanned out in front of me. There was nothing I couldn't tell him if I was willing to write long enough, and there was nothing he didn't at least try to understand and respond to.

This particular night I started writing to Breville about the garter snake that showed up in the kitchen. "It looks like it came in through a gap between the screen door and the frame," I said. "Once it got inside, it hid partway under the kitchen carpet. What always surprises me about snakes is how they are cool and dry to the touch—not slimy at all, the way some people think."

But pretty soon I switched subjects. In each letter I wrote Breville, I tried to process something about my rape. It was a way to remind myself of Breville's crime, but it was also a compulsion. I'd already gotten more out of writing to Breville than I had from any therapist, and I thought it was important to go on doing it. So this night I described my hometown. "I still make a trip back each year to visit my family, but the place is no longer home and hasn't been for a long, long time," I wrote. "After my rape, I used to hate to walk down the streets there. I was afraid the two men who had raped me would see me walking and either pull over to talk to me, or else start to jeer. The houses along South Tulpehocken Street, where my parents live, always have their blinds drawn to the street, but when I was a teenager those windows seemed like eyes. I thought the people who lived in the houses were watching me and gossiping about me, and I have never lost that feeling. The houses themselves are so close together that my parents can see into the kitchen of their neighbors and vice versa. There is nothing you can do that other people can't see. I think that is why I moved as soon as I could—to get away from prying and gossip."

After I put that all down, I lay thinking about my hometown and South Tulpehocken Street. And then, because I was thinking about my family, or maybe just because I hadn't spoken to anyone all day, I wrote Breville the story Merle had told me the other day, and that I had not been able to stop thinking about:

"He is the old man I rent the cabin from," I wrote. "His wife died less than a year ago, and of course he still misses her. She was only sixty-eight. He said she never wanted to move to town, not even as they got older and it got harder to take care of the house. She died when she was out in her garden last fall, getting it ready for winter. He said from what they could tell, she'd gotten cold and had built a little fire for herself, and she lay down beside it. He'd been away for the day, and when he got back, he was the one who found her. When I die I hope it's like that. I don't want to die slowly in a nursing home, the way my grandmother did. No thank you."

I knew it was morbid to talk about death, even if my vision was peaceful, and I knew it was ridiculous for me, a woman who was enjoying her life and her freedom, to write to a convict about dying. But that was what I was thinking about that night, and that was what I wanted to communicate to Breville. If he wanted to be my friend, he could be my friend, and he could go through a spell of sadness with me. So I folded the pages and tucked them into an envelope, and the next morning I mailed everything before I could make myself think better of it.

I'd told Breville before that letters were just pieces of paper, but of course that wasn't true. A power resides in a letter. There is the time that went into the writing of the pages and the fact that the writer actually touched the paper. There are also the secret, personal emanations that come from the way the words slant on the page, the depth to which a ballpoint pen has pressed, and the extravagance or precision with which vowels and consonants are shaped. That was why I kept the only letter a Jesuit priest wrote me when I was eighteen and living in New York City, after he had fallen in love with me on a bus, and why I still had some of the notes my high school girlfriends wrote me in math class, almost all of which were signed, *Love always.* I kept all those things not only for the sentiments expressed, but also because just seeing the handwriting made me remember the people and the time and the feeling of my own life. Not only were the letters evidence of old affections, but they were also artifacts—intimate mummy wrappings of friendships and love affairs. That is the best way I can explain what happened next, but all I really know is that after I sent the letter about dying, I wanted to meet Breville.

It wasn't because of how he responded to me, though he did write, *I can feel the peacefulness of the way that woman died by how you describe it and, yes, it is best to die the way you want, on your own terms. But I hope you don't think about it too much. About dying, I mean. I can't think of anyone who seems more filled with life than you.*

In fact I didn't think much about dying, and though I appreciated that Breville was attentive to what I'd written, whatever quiet sadness I felt that day had disappeared, evaporating like morning fog over the lake. But the feeling of wanting to meet him—that had been happening gradually and incrementally, and it remained.

I wanted to meet the person I had revealed so much to, and who had become, perhaps by default, the recipient of my observations and my dreams.

That person was Alpha Breville, resident of Stillwater state prison, convict, rapist, thief.

9

WHEN I FIRST SAW ALPHA BREVILLE in the visiting room at Stillwater, I did the same thing with him as I did with the old photo of
my dead thief: I studied him.

He was slight of build, with dark eyes and dark hair, and his
face was open. He wore a red and black western shirt that made
him look like a rodeo cowboy. I kept my eyes on him as I walked
toward a taped-off square of carpet, which was the only place in
all of the prison where visitors could touch inmates. A man and
woman had just embraced inside that square, there in front of the
guard who monitored body contact, but when Breville and I reached
the square, I only shook his hand.

The visiting room was nothing like those I'd seen on TV shows—
no glass separating inmates from visitors, no gray phone to pick up.
Breville and I sat in two plastic chairs that faced each other, at the
ends of two long rows of chairs. Bright sunlight streamed in the grilled
windows, and a spider plant hung above my head. If I moved a certain
way, one of the baby plants touched down on my hair.

"In the old days we could have sat beside each other," Breville
told me, and patted the empty chair next to his. "Then they
changed the visiting policy. Too many exchanges."

"What kind of exchanges?"

"Drugs," Breville said. "People passing things as they sat beside each other."

He stretched his legs out then, twisted each foot in its vinyl loafer. "I borrowed the shoes and the shirt. For the visit. I wanted to impress you. Didn't want you to see me in prison issue."

"I'm impressed that you borrowed clothes," I said. "You look like a cowboy."

"You probably think it's stupid."

"I don't," I said.

I listened to the small talk Breville made in those first minutes, and I made some of my own, but mostly I watched Breville's face and hands, and how he held his body, and in those first moments of conversation I came to understand something. It was something I had no way of knowing until I was in Breville's presence, until just that moment in the visiting room, when I was sitting face-to-face with him. And what I came to understand was this: Alpha Breville did not look like a rapist.

I know it is laughable to say that, because a rapist is anybody and can look like anyone, but I will say it again: Alpha Breville did not look like a rapist.

To begin with, there was his handsomeness. I wasn't prepared for his handsomeness, or how it pleased me to look at his face. His dark eyes glinted with understanding, and his whole body contained a spirit, an eagerness for life, which not even the visiting room at Stillwater state prison could crush. He was so young and handsome and gallant, and he carried himself with such a mixture of humility and strength, that at that moment it seemed absolutely clear to me there had been some mistake in his life, some set of events that had gone awry that led him to rape a woman in South Minneapolis. If he had been ugly or roughly put together or even unremarkable in his expression, if I had not felt drawn to him so strongly, I don't know what my assessment of him would have been. But none of those things was true, and at that moment I knew that if I had met Alpha Breville in any other place—at a bar or getting off a bus on Lake Street—I would have wanted something with him or from him.

And because it seemed so impossible that Breville was a rapist, it also became clear to me in an instant that if anyone, anyone at all, had helped Breville when he was growing up, he would not have turned out to be who he was. He had only been nineteen when he broke into that house, not so far out of his formative years and the stupidity of being a teenager, and if he did what he did, it was because someone had failed him. Of course, I knew not all callowness and immaturity ended in violence—it was one thing to break into a house and rob, and another to shove your unwanted cock into a woman's vagina, and Breville himself told me he'd been filled with violence when he was nineteen. But in that first hour of the visit, it was almost impossible for me to believe Breville had committed the crime for which he was incarcerated. I kept thinking that as Breville and I sat talking, and in a little while I told him my theory of his youth, because I could not go on sitting across from him without saying it.

"That's where you have it wrong, Suzanne," Breville said. "Lots of people tried to help. My mom, my dad. My grandfather. It didn't make any difference. I did it. I raped that woman."

I watched him as he said those words, and I had no choice but to believe them. Breville himself would not let me believe anything else. Yet even when I reminded myself that Breville was seven years into a fourteen-year sentence, that who I saw in front of me was a different person, almost entirely, than the one who had raped, everything about Breville seemed to belie his crime. It wasn't just his appearance, either. His self-awareness and honesty seemed genuine and more than just products of the prison 12-step programs he'd written me about in letters. When he said, *I did it, I raped that woman,* he looked away at first and then made himself look back at me—so I could study his face, it seemed. So I could know exactly who was sitting across from me.

When I kept shaking my head, when I told Breville how hard it was for me to put his crime together with his face, he said, "I'm glad you can see the person I am now. I don't think you would have liked me before, but I've changed. You know, I've been sober for seven years now."

Sitting there in the visiting room among the other inmates and their visitors, I understood for the first time what it might have taken for Breville to make the choices he had made in prison to get his associate's degree and work as many hours as he could. It was the smart thing to do, and by behaving that way, Breville curried favor for himself, but none of it would have been sustainable if he hadn't actually been changing. Or maybe I just came up with that rationalization because I wanted to believe the man I saw in front of me was the real Breville.

"You could have done your time in a harder way," I said. "From what you told me, I know that."

"True. But there's a reason I'm sitting here. There's a reason I'm sitting here and you're sitting there. I committed the crime."

After he said that, we were quiet for a little while. Breville stretched his legs and I brushed at the spider plant touching my hair, but in a moment we both sat still. It sounds clichéd to say, but we looked into each other's eyes. Regarded each other across the space of the aisle. We were in a public room, I was not sitting close to Breville, and I'd only touched his hand briefly when we greeted each other in front of the guard, but I still had a sense of Breville's presence, as I am sure he had a sense of mine. I could feel a sadness in the moment and in the air between us in the visiting room of Stillwater state prison, but underlying that impression was also a feeling of peace. I do not know any other way to say it. I felt calm in Breville's presence, and the quietness between us did not feel awkward or self-conscious.

"What kind of swimming have you been doing?" Breville asked me after a little while. As he said it he leaned forward slightly and moved his chin up once, encouraging me to talk. It wasn't lost on me that he was the one trying to lead us out of silence—it was usually my role with students or with the taciturn men I dated.

"I swim across the lake a couple times a week. Whenever it's quiet," I said. "This week someone in a boat told me I should be wearing a flag."

"What did you say?"

"I wanted to tell him he should put a flag on his beer, but I didn't," I said, and Breville laughed at that. Then it was easy enough to talk.

Strangely, or perhaps not so strangely, some of that first visit had the giddiness of a date. Though outside of that taped-off square Breville and I were not allowed to touch, if we both sat forward in our chairs we could talk quietly and intently, so much so that the distance between us seemed only like the distance between a man and a woman at a table in a restaurant. Still, toward the end of the two hours—after we had a picture taken together by the trustee with a Polaroid who worked in the visiting room—something happened that showed just how much of a wall existed between us.

"Did they search you when you came in?" Breville asked.

When I looked at him, puzzled, he said, "They must not have."

"What do you mean?"

"I get strip-searched every time I get a visitor. Before and after. I have to bend over and crack a smile."

When I didn't say anything, he said, "You don't know what that means, do you?"

I shook my head no, and he said, "I have to spread the cheeks of my ass apart for the guards. I just wondered if they did it to you, too."

I thought at first it was rudeness or stupidity that made him ask the question, but I knew from his letters that Breville was anything but stupid. That made me wonder even more. Why hadn't he ever asked another of his visitors, if he'd wanted to know? And did he really think that because I was coming to see him, the guards would have power over me, too?

"I'm not the one who did anything wrong," I said. "Besides, I wouldn't go through it."

Breville nodded. "I don't blame you," he said, and then he looked away from me. When he looked away, I wondered if he hadn't known the answer all along, if he hadn't said what he said because he wanted to see my reaction. When I thought that, I could feel my expression change and go hard. In another second, though, Breville was thanking me for making the trip down to Stillwater, and he seemed so sincere I couldn't maintain the coldness in my eyes.

When I said goodbye to Breville that first day, I wasn't going to hug him, but after we got to the taped-off square where inmates could touch and be touched, that was what I ended up doing. I put my arms quickly around Breville and felt his arms go around me. I felt his body against mine. I thought I would be able to smell him, some kind of sour prison smell, or at least the scent of his hair, but I smelled nothing. I pulled away and said goodbye.

1 0

THE SISTER OF MY RAPIST was a girl I went to school with. We often sat together in classes and in homerooms because our last names started with the same letter. Joy was tough, part of a crowd of kids who were hoods from the time of fifth or sixth grade. If you had parents that were certain kinds of people—drunks and toughs, or just poor bastards—you had to be part of that crowd. Some kids might have chosen the crowd out of wanting to be "tuff," the way it was spelled on the bathroom walls at school, but many people had no choice. Joy didn't. Her brothers made a name for themselves and the family with drinking and drugs, and charges like assault and possession.

I did not know if Joy's brothers were ever nice to her or what her family was like; neither of us talked much about home. When we sat together in Mrs. Sander's room, Joy sometimes told me how her mom and dad were fighting, or how her dad had been drinking, but that was no different from what my parents did, or many parents did. But something made Joy's family different. Each of Joy's three brothers had the same eyes, and each was wild and bad. The brothers were not clannish—there was enough difference in their ages for them not to run together—but you just had to say the name

L—— and people knew, or believed they knew. What do you expect in a small Pennsylvania town, a deer-hunting and coal-mining town, where nothing anyone does is hidden from anyone else?

Joy was the toughest girl and I was one of the smartest, and we both liked that we were friends with each other, that we could be friends across the lines that divided us, even at that age. We were like heads of state when we talked about girls in our grade, or school, or her boyfriends, and we listened to each other so carefully we were solemn. I was sitting at my desk in Mrs. Sander's room close to the end of seventh grade when Joy turned back to talk to me.

"It's serious," she said. "I have to talk to you."

"What's it about?"

"I can't say here. It's George," she said. "I'll tell you in gym."

As she leaned back over my desk to whisper just that much, I could smell the strange pepper smell on her breath that she carried each day. It was not a bad smell, but I didn't know where it came from.

Joy and I were sitting on the hard benches of the girls' locker room, away from the other girls, when she told me she thought she might be pregnant.

"How late are you?"

"Two weeks."

"You might or might not be," I said. "Do you use something?"

"No," she told me. "He just pulls out."

"That doesn't work," I said. I'd read about it. "It just takes a little bit."

Joy nodded. "I know."

"Maybe you're not," I said, though I didn't know how that could be. I wasn't having sex yet—just fingerfucking and messing around—but I knew how everything worked, and I felt scared for Joy. The idea of sex frightened me. Part of me couldn't believe Joy was doing it already, and part of me wondered how she got un-scared.

I sat with Joy until Miss Harvath blew her whistle for all of us to come out into the gym. I didn't know what had made Joy tell me instead of one of her other friends, but I think it was this: whenever she talked to me, whatever it was about, I always listened with my whole self. Perhaps that sounds stupid, but I do not think it was. Think how seldom anyone listened to you when you were thirteen.

It turned out Joy was not pregnant. She and George waited for me outside the middle school one morning to tell me. George was old enough to drive, and he brought Joy in early to school. They both were waiting in the misty morning for me to come up walking.

"I got it," she said. She was hanging on to George's jacket, one of her hands digging down into his pocket.

"That's good," I said. "Now you don't have to worry."

Joy pushed George away from her then and told him, "Go on. Kiss her."

George walked toward me, put his arms around me, and kissed me on the mouth. It caught me by surprise. I didn't know why Joy wanted him to do it or why he would do such a thing—maybe be-cause I knew so much about the two of them, or maybe because it was a dare. Or perhaps Joy wanted to prove something to him: that I wasn't a snob, and that she could procure me for him. I didn't know. I accepted the kiss.

Later on, when the two of them had some kind of fight, Joy made George call me on the phone to find out if she had been cheating or not. It was summer and I hadn't seen Joy since school let out, but I knew what to say, and I believed it.

"No," I said. "She would never cheat. She is the best person I know."

"Never?" George asked.

"It's you she loves."

I was some kind of final witness, a barometer of truth.

When Joy and I got to high school, she was exploratory and I was college prep, so we didn't have homeroom together anymore, and there was no class we had in common. Yet we continued to be friends, if distantly, and when some girls began to call my house, accusing me of everything from stuffing my bra to thinking I was better than everyone else, it was Joy I went to.

"Who do you think it is?" she asked me when I got done telling her what was going on.

"I know one of them is Cheryl Korr. But I always hear two voices on the phone."

"It's probably that Jane Zimmerman. What do they say to you?"

"They say, 'We don't like the way you act.'"

"They don't even know you."

"I don't know how else I'm supposed to act. I'm just being myself."

"Cheryl doesn't have any guts anyway," Joy said. "I'll talk to them. Next time I see them in the bathroom."

And I knew she had done it, because one afternoon Jane Zimmerman called, crying, saying she was sorry.

"I didn't want to make those calls to you," she said. "I didn't want to hurt you. It was Cheryl's idea."

No one called my house again.

The truth was I did think I was better than some people in my school. Certainly better than beefy Cheryl Korr. But I did not think I was better than everyone, and I did not think I was better than Joy. Which was why the next thing that happened bothered me so much, though I told myself it needn't. No one else ever knew about it. It started with me and ended with me.

It happened one day in early spring of tenth grade. I was walking down the hall at school and saw Joy coming toward me. I don't know if I noticed from a long way off, or if it took me a few seconds to see.

Months earlier, I'd gone through my closet to get together old clothes to sell at the thrift shop in town. One of the things I got rid of was a long-sleeved black shirt with a keyhole neckline. I loved the shirt in seventh grade, but once my breasts got bigger, my mother told me it looked obscene and I felt funny wearing it.

That was the shirt Joy was wearing this particular day. My old shirt. It still had the button at the keyhole neck sewn with white thread, the crummy fix-up job I'd done when I was too lazy to find a spool of black. The shirt was tight on Joy, too, but that was part of the way she dressed: low hip-hugger jeans and tight shirts.

I told myself she never would have bought the shirt if she remembered me wearing it in the seventh grade, if she had known it used to be mine. I told myself it didn't really matter where people got their clothes from anyway. Still, I felt funny that the shirt made its way to her, that she was getting her clothing from the thrift shop on South Main.

"Hey, Suzanne," Joy said when we drew near each other in the hall, while I was staring at that button with white thread. I could tell she'd seen me startle, but her face was not angry or embarrassed. Only puzzled.

"Hey, Joy," I said back, and we kept on walking to get to class before the bell rang.

The night I was raped, my boyfriend Cree was doing one of his disappearing acts. He'd stood me up for a date earlier in the week—left me sitting on the front steps, looking up and down the street, waiting for his green car to come driving up. When he didn't bother to even call to apologize, I told myself there were other places I could go for what he gave. I wasn't the same girl I'd been in seventh grade: when Cree stood me up, I not only had hurt feelings, but I also had to suppress all the sexual imagining I'd been

doing for days. I loved Cree's body so much, and I liked all the
places we had sex: an old mine road in Ravine; a meadow up on
895, where the Appalachian Trail ran; beside an abandoned farmhouse in Deturksville, where we liked to take a blanket under the
dogwoods. Sometimes, in the night air, dogwood petals would fall
on us.

Keil Ward had wild blond hair and blue eyes that slanted up at
the outsides—or maybe it was just his high cheekbones that made
it seem that way. He was one of the men who flirted with me constantly when he saw me at the restaurant where I waited tables, and
he always asked me to go out with him after I got off my shifts. This
particular night, after Cree stood me up and a week before my seven-
teenth birthday, I finally said yes to him, and after my shift, it was
Keil Ward who waited for me in the side hallway of the restaurant.

When we walked to his truck he slipped his arm around me,
and it thrilled me—he smelled different from Cree, and he was
taller and heavier. I wanted to know what it would be like to touch
him. I wondered what his shoulders and chest would feel like when
we embraced, and I wondered what his mouth tasted like. He
kissed my hair as we were walking and it felt good to have him pay
attention to me. I didn't see the other person sitting in his truck
until he opened the door. Then I saw.

"This is my friend Frank," Keil told me. "You don't mind if
we drop him off, do you?"

I paused for one second and then Keil was lifting me into the
truck and Frank L—— was reaching for me.

In truth, I didn't know much about Frank L——. I knew his
name and that he was the oldest in Joy's family. He sat drinking
every night at the bar of the restaurant, but he never talked to me.
He looked a little like Joy, though I do not like to think of his face. He
was twenty-seven, eleven years older than I was. Before he raped
me, he kissed me and chewed at my pussy. Then he fucked me so

hard he made small tears in my vagina, and the skin of my labia bruised and turned black. I don't know if it would have made a difference to him if he knew I was a friend of his sister, if he would have gone through with it all.

Even though Keil Ward set the thing up, even though he was the one who tricked me, I never called him my rapist. He held me for Frank, pushed the hair from my face when Frank wanted to see—but he didn't fuck me. He didn't hurt my vagina. I sucked his cock while Frank was fucking me, but that didn't hurt. Keil's jeans smelled like bleach and his penis tasted like medicine. He was the one who helped me get dressed at the end.

In a couple days, it hurt to walk, and I knew I had to tell someone what had happened. So I talked to my French teacher and she took me to the hospital. That's when I found out I had herpes and gonorrhea. But there was no gun, no knife. Just Frank L——and his cock.

11

AS IT TURNED OUT, Breville was the one who smelled me that day at the prison. I didn't get the letter for a couple of days, but the evening after our first visit, he wrote me, *We're deprived of smells in here, so maybe we're more sensitive. All I know is that after you left I could still smell you on my clothes. I cannot tell you what it meant that you came to see me.*

I hadn't worn perfume, so Breville must have smelled the lotion I'd put on after my bath, or my shampoo, or their mix on my skin and hair. Or maybe he simply smelled the me-ness of me. All I knew was that I felt alarmed and self-conscious about the whole thing. It made me feel funny to know my scent had such a profound effect on Breville, but I knew most of what I was responding to was Breville's bluntness: he had smelled me. Whatever the smell had been composed of hardly mattered—the scent was mine, and Breville now knew that intimate thing about me. I felt embarrassed. Vulnerable. It reminded me of being in seventh grade and the first time I let my seventh-grade boyfriend work his fingers up into my vagina. Afterward, when we were walking out of the woods where we'd fooled around, he told me, "I can smell you on my fingers." I thought it was bad that my vagina had a smell, but then I saw him

keep finding ways to put his hand up to his face, and I didn't
worry so much.

After the initial panic I felt reading Breville's letter, other thoughts
began to surface. I'd been caught off guard by the intimacy of what
he'd written—he had *smelled* me—but there was something forthright
about the revelation. His words had a directness I hadn't encountered
on any number of dates with men who'd answered my ad: a young
engineer who wanted a woman to spend time with him on his boat on
Lake Minnetonka, and who was so lonely that the void in his life made
his face tense and brooding; a gold trader who was smooth and amorous on the first date, pressing his erection into my belly upon saying
goodnight, but who made excuses every time thereafter about why he
couldn't go to a museum or out to dinner with me; or even the grave
digger, whom I actually met for coffee, and who appraised me by saying, "You look pretty good even if you do have a few miles on you."

I told myself that if my scent had such a strong effect on Breville,
it didn't mean I was vulnerable, but rather that I had power. I had
power over Breville not only because I could stop everything and
never again come to Stillwater state prison to see him, but also because of what I represented. I was a conduit for the entire outside
world, or at least the bits of it I could carry on my skin and clothing. I felt as though I embodied an entire sense, and the idea flattered me. I decided the next time I went to visit, I would wear
perfume. I didn't usually wear any fragrance in summer—I thought
it was cloying in the heat—but I'd tolerate it for Breville and wear
Saint Laurent's Paris, sweet chemical rose. It would give Breville
something special to smell, and I could hide behind the fragrance.

Perfume. Colored water in a bottle. It seemed like a small
enough thing to do, to plan to give Breville a scent to smell. But of
course it wasn't. It meant something had changed between Breville
and me, though it took me a couple of days to realize it.

His pleasure had become important to me.

12

NEXT WEEK when I drove the four hours down to the Cities from the cabin, I stopped at the rest area in Rogers and doused myself with perfume. When I walked into the visitors' waiting room at Stillwater, the scent was so heavy I was sure everyone would look at me as I passed by, but no one did. Each person in that room had his or her mind on private thoughts, I knew, but it soon became clear that I was not notable enough to draw anyone's attention in that place. Though I couldn't smell anything except Paris, I figured I wasn't the only woman there wearing too much perfume, and as far as drawing attention—well, that honor went to a young woman with long, dark hair using what appeared to be a silver drum major's baton as a cane. She wore a skimpy dress with spaghetti straps, and she had a rough, hacking cough that made her seem old, even though she was probably just twenty, or perhaps still in her teens. I couldn't believe my eyes when I saw her, and I was so fascinated by her tubercular cough and the troubled craziness she projected that when she got up to go to the bathroom, I waited a few moments and then followed. She was already in a stall when I entered, so I stood fiddling with my hair until she exited. To wash her hands, she leaned her drum major's baton against the wall, but before she could even get the faucet turned on, she had to hack into her fist.

"That's some cough you have," I said. "It sounds like it hurts."

"I'd get better faster if I stopped smoking," she told me, but I could tell from the way her voice sounded she didn't want to speak to me, didn't want to share a girls' moment in the bathroom.

"It's hard to quit," I said, keeping on, in part because I wanted to go on looking at her.

"I've tried."

I would have gone on staring at her, but she took her baton in hand and clumped and clicked out of the bathroom. I was left standing on my own in the cool green-tiled room, so I peed and took a while washing my hands so it wouldn't seem as if I were following her. When I got out into the waiting room, I meant to listen to see what inmate name was called that would cause her to rise and walk to the guard's station, but in the end I failed even to do that because I couldn't keep the names straight as the intercom announced, "Visit for ——, visit for ——." That's the way the guards did it—they would call the name of the inmate or inmates who had visitors, not the visitors' names. It protected the privacy of those in the waiting room and drew all attention to the men who were incarcerated. All I knew for certain was the young woman got called before the guards announced my "Visit for Breville," and I watched her negotiate to have her drum major's baton returned to her after she passed through the metal detector. Whatever malady of ankle or foot she cited, requiring her to use a cane but still permitting her to wear high-heeled shoes, worked, and she tapped her way into the locked cage between the waiting room and the prison.

Watching all of that unfold, as well as observing all the wives and girlfriends waiting to see whatever incarcerated male they'd come to see, did something to me that day. I thought, *You have become a joke, Suzanne, you have become like those women in super-*

market magazines who fall for convicts, who have so few prospects that they pick a prison suitor. I felt so foolish I wondered if I should stand up and walk out of the huge wooden doors, more like doors to a church than a prison. But I did not get up and leave. That was another part of my foolishness. Still, I swore if I felt the same way at the end of the visit as I did at that moment, I would never come back to Stillwater state prison.

I was still thinking that and doubting myself and my actions as I passed through the locking cage door and walked toward Breville and the taped square where we could embrace in front of the guards. Because we had hugged goodbye at the end of the last visit, it seemed we had to again repeat the gesture to greet each other today, and when I touched Breville, it felt utterly false to me, and I wondered why I was doing it. Breville's shoulders and back felt odd, rigid and unknown, and why wouldn't they? He was an absolute stranger to me. But I couldn't stop myself from making the gesture—I didn't know how not to. And in those seconds when we were embracing, when my arms were around Breville so woodenly and his were around me, he said into my hair, on the side of me that faced away from the guards, "You smell so good. Jesus Christ, so sweet."

And again I was disarmed.

Even though the feeling of falseness and rigidity was still there, even though I did not feel any natural warmth for Breville, I was glad I hadn't resisted the embrace, insisting only on a handshake. A refusal like that would have created an awkwardness that I didn't want to put him or myself through.

And oddly, within seconds of taking our places in facing chairs at the end of two rows there in the visiting room of Stillwater state prison, things began to feel more normal. Maybe because the moment in front of the guards was over, maybe because we were able to walk together that short distance, to the end of the rows of chairs—I don't know. I just know that as I sat down, the room began to feel familiar to me, and it began to feel ordinary to be sitting across the aisle from Breville with the spider plant again touching down on my hair if I shifted too far to the left. Whatever hesitation and misgiving I had felt in the waiting room, and whatever uneasiness I had felt when I was touching Breville—those things had all passed. And I think they passed because it became immediately clear to me how genuinely moved Breville was to see me. I couldn't remember a time someone looked happier to be in my presence.

"Tell me what it's called," he said, leaning forward into the aisle, sitting on the edge of his chair.

"What what's called?"

"Your perfume."

"Paris," I said.

"It's nice," he said. "It suits you."

I nodded at that but didn't say anything, and we sat there, not talking for a little while. Just looking across the aisle at each other, taking the other person in. And if you can believe that it felt natural to be sitting in a room with cages on the windows and being watched by any number of prison guards, then perhaps you will be able to understand when I say I felt some kind of pure happiness just then.

For most of the two-hour visit, Breville and I didn't say anything of consequence, not about his crime or my rape. Instead we talked about places we had traveled and adventures we'd had. He couldn't believe I'd been to Kadoka, that I'd spent a night in Interior, South Dakota, that I'd eaten shrimp at the same fry shack where he'd had many dinners in the summers, or that I knew exactly which Happy Chef Restaurant he'd bused tables at when he was fifteen and desperate for cash.

When I told him about the place I'd grown up in, I said, "It's probably not all that different from Kadoka, except it has the Appalachian Mountains around it."

"Tell me about someplace else, then," Breville said. "Anyplace that isn't like Kadokah. You don't ever want to go back there, do you?"

"No, I don't want to go back."

So I told him instead about the month I'd spent in Nice when I was twenty, and about how the beach was all rocks, and about how I'd nearly drowned one evening when I went into the sea and the water was rolling hard at the drop-off. It had taken all my strength to break free of the turning.

"How many oceans have you swum in?"

"The Mediterranean, the Adriatic, the Atlantic, and the Pacific."

"I was once to the Pacific," Breville said. "Never the Atlantic. But I swam the Missouri and the Mississippi."

"I'm saltwater but I knew you were fresh," I said, and he laughed, as I'd meant him to.

"Do you think it was fated that we meet?" Breville asked.

"I'm not sure."

"I think it was fated. I don't know how else it could have happened. I'm a thief and a rapist, and look at you. Look at what you are."

"What am I?"

"You know what you are. How else could we have come together?"

"I don't want to believe it was fated that I relive my rape," I said. "If that's fate, I'm not interested."

"I'm sorry. You know I didn't mean that part of it."

"I think it's more likely coincidence," I told Breville. "I don't know. What does your hand say? What do the lines of your hand say?"

I showed him then from across the aisle the little horizontal lines under the side of the pinky finger that supposedly indicated the number of serious relationships or marriages a person had. I had two lines, but Breville had three.

"You're more fickle than I am," I said.

"Which is the life line?"

"The one that snakes down your palm and wraps under the thumb," I said. "Here are the heart line and the head line," I said, again showing him my hand, tracing the lines. "And that's my psychic cross."

"What is?"

"This cross," I said, and I sat as far forward in my chair as I could and traced the intersecting lines at the center of my palm.

He leaned close to see as I lightly carved out the cross. He reached out a hand then, and for the briefest of seconds he touched the center of my cross with his index finger.

"Breville, to the guard."

His name seemed to be called at the exact moment he touched me, and quickly I realized that we were watched closely. Breville sighed and stood up and walked toward the guard's table.

When he came back to the chair, he was carrying a small white slip of paper.

"Are you in trouble?"

"It's just a warning," he said.

"I'm sorry. I'm sorry."

"It isn't your fault. I knew better."

And though he tucked the slip into his pocket, it took a moment longer to push it from his mind and compose his face.

"It doesn't mean anything, Suzanne. It's just a write-up."

And then they called, "Breville, five minutes," and I knew I would have to leave soon.

When Breville and I hugged in the taped square that day, it still felt awkward to me. Though I felt the warmth of his body, there was no ease in the embrace, no naturalness. With any other man

I'd spent so much time talking and writing to, I would have already had an intimate knowledge—sex was a way I got to know a man, not a culmination. But with Breville there was nothing. As I held him I couldn't get over the idea that I didn't know anything about his body—not the way his chest curved into his belly, not the way the muscles of his thighs were braided, not the feeling of his scalp under my fingers—nothing. Even though I'd thought Breville was good-looking from the first time I'd come to Stillwater, I hadn't thought of touching him until that moment. But just then I wanted nothing so much as to kiss him and find out what his mouth tasted like. If my lips even touched Breville's, though, let alone if we'd French-kissed and touched tongues, he'd get thrown in the hole. The hole—he'd told me that was the punishment, solitary confinement for a kiss.

But I felt concern for him, over the white slip of paper and for what I knew his life to be, and that was part of my embrace that day. I know I tried to let that feeling travel out through my arms and breasts and hands. And I believe Breville must have felt it from me, because when we parted and began walking away—him back to his cell and me back to the locking cage and the waiting room—we both turned to look at the other. I nodded a few times and tried to show something with my eyes, and Breville did the same, nodding and saying goodbye with his eyes, and then he put his hand out at waist level, palm down, and made a smooth pass through the air, as if to say he was fine, that whatever feelings he had were smoothed over, that he was steady. That he would remain so until I came again.

In the air in front of the guards, that was what he told me with no words.

13

IN HIGH SCHOOL, Cree and I usually parked out at Brommer's old farmhouse, but a week after I was raped, we broke into the Boy Scout camp in Rock.

It was Cree's idea. He wanted the night to be special, I think. All week I asked my mom to tell him I wasn't home when he called, and I think he was worried he was losing me. Or maybe he just wanted to be with me someplace new.

All the way out there, I kept thinking, *I should tell him now, I should get it over with.* I practiced it over and over, but I couldn't say it. The word rape wasn't even in my mind because I thought I had brought everything on myself when I consented to go out with Keil Ward. If I had done what I was supposed to and stayed at home like a good and faithful girlfriend, nothing bad would have happened and I wouldn't be sitting there with a raw and seeping vagina.

I knew I had to at least tell Cree about the infections. And yet I could not bring myself to say those words, either.

"Did you miss me this week?" he asked as we took the dirt road up to the cabins. The road twisted through the woods and the trees met overhead. The forest went for miles out there.

"I missed you," I said.

"Thought you were still mad at me."

"I was. But not anymore." I didn't say that it seemed like a long time ago that I was mad at him for disappearing, for not calling. It didn't seem to matter anymore.

"Come here," Cree said, and I slid beneath his arm. It was good to have him touching me, to be driving on the quiet black road.

At the camp all the cabins were padlocked but Cree used his knife to slip open the hook of a shutter on one of the windows. He climbed in easily, but I had to boost myself up on my hands first and then swing my leg up onto the sill. I waited there for a second for some of the burning to stop.

"Let's find a bunk with a mattress," Cree said when I got inside.

I could hear him moving in the cabin but couldn't see him.

"Here. Here's one."

I followed his voice and then lay down with him on the narrow bunk. I tried to act like nothing was wrong, like things were the way they always were. I slipped my arms around him and let one hand rest at his hip, one on his back.

We kissed for a long time and it soothed me. The air in the cabin was damp and musty, but when the breeze came in through the opened shutter, I could smell the woods. The smell wasn't just pine—it was the smell of all the trees and the leaves mixed together. A green smell. I wished I could just be there with nothing on my mind, just smelling the green and holding Cree.

I couldn't, though. When he pulled away from me and reached for my jeans, I stopped him.

"I can't," I said.

"What, do you have your period?"

I could feel his hand resting on the soft part of my belly, waiting. For a second I thought I might tell him. I got afraid of the words again, though, and could only nod. I knew he couldn't see me in the darkness.

"It doesn't matter if there's blood," he said. "You know that."

He waited a second and then started to open my jeans again. That time I pushed his hand away. Even in the darkness I knew he was watching me.

I still didn't say anything. But I moved away from him so that I was lying beside him rather than underneath, and then I moved again so I was the one on top. I moved down over his body and he pressed up against me, but I didn't let him reach for me. Instead I unbuttoned his shirt and kissed his belly. Slipped down his jeans.

After Cree came in my mouth, we lay together. He kept touching my face, kept wrapping his hands in my hair. I listened to the wind outside in the trees and then stood up to get a tissue from my pocket.

"You all right?"

"I'm okay," I said.

"You sure?"

"It just makes my nose run."

If Cree thought anything was strange about my refusal to fuck, he never said. He was used to my moodiness, and maybe he thought it was that, or maybe he thought it was connected to my period, or maybe he was just content to come in my mouth.

"Did you get your dress yet?"

"I'm going to pick it up Friday," I said. Our prom was a week away, and I was having someone make my dress because I didn't want one of the frilly affairs the stores were selling. I wanted a black halter instead. "I have to wait to get my paycheck on Thursday," I said.

"You need money?"

"I'll have enough. Besides, you're paying for everything else."

"Well, let me know if you need it."

He held my hand as we drove back to town. "Are you glad we came?" he asked.

I knew what he meant, but for a second I thought, *Well, you're the only one who came.* It wasn't his fault—I was to blame, and an orgasm was the last thing on my mind—but I still thought it. But instead I said, "You know I am."

I moved over to sit close to him, and that's when I decided I would never tell him what had happened or what I'd done. I knew I could take care of everything myself. It was easier to protect him by giving him blow jobs. That way he wouldn't have to know, I wouldn't have to tell, and everything could stay the same.

As it turned out, we broke up a few weeks after prom anyway. In spite of my oral skills and secrecy, nothing stayed the same.

1 4

THE CASINO was called the Northern Lights but the name was a
misnomer: the only aurora came from the parking lot floodlights
that turned the night sky gray. I arrived just as the band was climb-
ing down from the stage in the big outdoor tent and going on a
break, so even though I didn't care to gamble, I joined the crush of
people coming and going through the casino door. It felt odd to be
in the woods and in a crowd at the same time, and the combination
took me by surprise.

The jackpot slots near the door were crowded with nickel players and the bar was crowded, too. Despite that initial crush,
though, farther back inside the casino, there was only a smattering
of people, tourists mostly. I'd come out to hear music, be among
people and have a drink, so I circled back to the front and found a
Double Diamond slot kitty-corner from the bar. I hadn't even bothered to get quarters when I came in—I was waiting for the band to
start again and didn't want to be stuck with a cup full of coins—but
I had some in my wallet, leftover from doing laundry, and I began
to play them. In a few minutes I flagged down a waiter.

"Vodka tonic. Absolut if you have it."

"We have it."

"Busy night?"

"Crazy. But it's always crazy when there's a band."

"I like your shirt," I said then. "Very Minnesotan. Very north woods."

He laughed then because it was a tropical, Hawaiian-looking thing he was wearing.

"At least I don't have to wear that," he said, motioning to the blackjack dealers, who were all sporting purple tuxedo shirts and bow ties.

"Yeah, you got the better end of the deal," I said, looking at the triangle of skin that showed in his open collar. It was smooth.

"I'll be right back with your drink."

In a couple minutes, I spent all the quarters I'd walked in with, but I'd also gotten thirty credits, which allowed me to go on playing.

"Here you go, miss."

When I took the drink from the waiter's hand, I said, "Want to hear a joke?"

"A joke? Sure."

"I'm what you would call a social drinker. When someone says, 'I think I'll have a drink,' I say, 'Then so shall I.'"

He laughed then—genuinely, it seemed, or maybe it was also just part of his job.

I put two dollars on his serving tray. "I'm going outside and hear the music," I said. "Thanks."

"People are having a good time out there," he said, and again I watched his throat, the smooth skin of his neck. I was older than he was. I wondered if it mattered.

It had been warm inside the casino, but it was even warmer outside—a moist Minnesota night. In spite of the heat, as soon as the band started playing again, people moved out onto the dance floor. I stood on the left side of the stage, listening and watching, but in a little while I was dancing, too. In my own spot, by myself, but swaying to the songs even if I wasn't on the dance floor. I didn't mind. I was in a throng, there were people's faces to watch and music to hear, and that was all I really wanted.

When I saw a few people in leather vests work their way onto the floor from the opposite side of the tent, I didn't think much of it—for all I knew, bikers liked Cajun music, too. But everyone on the floor seemed to clear a path for these particular dancers, and there was some kind of buzz about their presence that made me look again at them. When the bikers got close enough, I was able to read the patches on their vests, and then I understood the berth everyone was giving.

I hadn't even known there were such people as Minnesota Free-men, but there they were on the dance floor, men and women, drinks in hand. It hadn't been so long since the sieges at Ruby Ridge and Waco—I could see all of it registering on people's faces as they read the jackets. Those who didn't know were told by those who did, but no one said anything to the Freemen, who were laugh-ing and drinking beers and dancing like everyone else. In a little while the crowd absorbed the Freemen, or at least closed around them, and we were all there together, sweating and dancing—white tourists and Anishinabe Indians, north woods longhairs, loggers, county workers, and now the militia. All yelling and laughing and drinking, along with the band up from Louisiana.

But there was a wariness among us. The Freemen had brought it out, and I could see it in people's faces. For a while I got the feel-ing anything might happen: a knife pulled, a punch thrown, some-thing worse. But nothing did happen, and the longer it went on not happening, the more people relaxed and accepted that it would not happen. People looked at the Freemen, but the Freemen chose not to notice or were so used to it they didn't care. They kept to themselves, their men dancing with their women, only talking to each other. The longer I watched them, the more I felt like I understood what they were doing there. The tent with its music and its loudness and light on that moist night was irresistible, and even the militia needed to take a break once in a while.

"Why aren't you out dancing? Why are you standing here?"

I didn't even have to turn to know who it was.

"I might ask you the same thing," I said to the waiter who'd brought me my vodka tonic. I saw he'd taken off his Hawaiian nightmare of a shirt and was now in a T-shirt and jeans. "I thought you were working," I said.

"I'm off," he said, lighting a cigarette. "And I already pulled a double shift, so they can't ask me to work again." When he saw me watching him smoke, he offered me his pack.

"No, thanks," I told him. "I'll take a dance instead."

He shook his head no, but when I took his hand and led him out onto the dance floor, he came willingly enough.

"What's your name?"

"Suzanne. What's yours?"

"Dallas."

"Like the old TV show or like the city?" I said, but he couldn't hear me. It didn't matter. It was easier not to talk, easier to jostle among the other dancers. And when the band played the next song, it was easier to stay on the dance floor, shuffling and swaying, than to make our way back to the edges of the standing crowd.

"That joke you told me," the waiter said between songs, leaning in close to talk directly into my ear. "That was a good one. I liked it."

"Did you?" I said. "I don't tell too many jokes."

"You told that one good."

The band picked a slow song to play next, and the waiter wrapped both arms around me like boys did in high school, and we were close to each other, turning in a small circle.

"So why?" the waiter said then into my hair.

"Why what?"

"Why did you tell me a joke? If you don't tell jokes?"

"You looked like you needed a joke just then."

He held me a little tighter after I said that. I kept my arms up on his shoulders in the same place, but I felt him all the same.

"Suzanne," he said at the end of the song. "Suzanne the social drinker. I need a beer. What about you?"

"Sure," I said. "I think there's a line, though." But he was already walking away.

I stayed on the dance floor, watching the band's lead singer in his white jeans, watching a couple of the Freemen as they danced with their long-haired women. Before I knew it, Dallas was back beside me, handing me a red plastic cup.

When I looked at him, I raised my eyebrows a little.

"I have connections," he told me, and laughed.

We were drinking those beers and dancing, lightly holding each other's free hand, when the band went into its final song of the set. It took us a moment to pick up on the lyrics, but when we did, the waiter downed his beer and set the cup on the ground to clap and holler. The lead singer in the band kept dropping all the dirty words—I guess that's how they got away with singing a song like that—but we got the message all the same:

Uncle Bud, Uncle Bud,
Uncle Bud's got this, Uncle Bud's got that.
Uncle Bud's got a —— like a baseball bat.
Uncle Bud, Uncle Bud.
Uncle Bud's got a wife, she's big and fat,
She's got a —— like a Stetson hat.
Uncle Bud, Uncle Bud.

The verses went on and on, and the crowd loved it. I could see from the waiter's face that he did, too. He was stomping his feet and clapping, and so was I.

Uncle Bud's a man, a man in full,
His —— hang down like a Louisiana mule.

After the song was done—after we all hollered and clapped the band into playing one more before they left the stage—the waiter asked me if I wanted to go for a walk. I let him take my hand and we walked away from the dance tent, out toward the parking lot.

"So, do you like working here?" I said as we were walking.

"It's a job," he said.

When I heard his voice, I realized it was a stupid question to ask, so I tried again.

"What do you do when you aren't working?"

"I hunt. I work on cars with my uncle."

Then we were standing beside his car and I let him pull me to him.

His kiss was warm and thorough, and I liked the bitter taste of smoke in his mouth. But even though I felt his urgency, I didn't feel any of my own. When I pulled away, I saw his wolfish face and almost relented—I thought maybe if I went on, I would feel something. I wanted to feel something. But I didn't, and I suddenly didn't feel like trying.

I said, "I can't."

He looked at me for a second and then he came at me again. And I let him. Part of me wanted to fuck—I felt it inside me, brought on by the dancing and the vodka and beer and not least of all the lewd song, but I didn't want to go home with a stranger and try to please him. I wanted to go back to the cabin and lie in bed in a cotton nightgown.

"I'm sorry," I said when I pulled away the second time. "My heart's not in it."

He brushed the back of one hand over my breasts. "Yeah," he said. "I'm not so much interested in your heart."

"But I am," I said, and we stood looking at each other in the parking lot light.

"Jesus," was all he said, and then I was walking away from him.

Something in me felt fragile as I turned—my back felt tight—but I kept going, first toward the casino and then to the opposite end of the parking lot where I'd parked. The band had one more set to play, I knew, but I'd heard enough. Seen enough.

When I got back home and pulled up beside the cabin, I wished I'd left a light on for myself. I felt a little empty, deflated somehow. Once I got inside, though, everything was just the way I'd left it: the jar of Merle's peonies on the table, the quilt neatly covering the couch. And then I wasn't empty or sorry. I was glad to be alone. I knew it wasn't the waiter I wanted, it was the idea of a man I wanted. His kiss, his mouth on me, the wing of his collarbone and the pouch of his balls. But I didn't know the man I wanted, and my wanting didn't make him real.

After I washed my face and got in bed, I stayed up a long time reading. The air was so warm and moist I only needed the sheet over me, and I was glad not to be working over the waiter's body in the heat, dipping my head to suck his cock or taking him up into my cunt. Back at the casino I thought it was odd that I didn't want to bring him home, but now that I was back here, it wasn't surprising at all, and I found myself remembering something an old friend had told me a long time ago. *If you can't go to bed with someone who's read a good book*, she said, *just go to bed with a book*.

Still, I knew I had come close to fucking Dallas, though whether out of loneliness or the need to prove I was a participant in life, I couldn't say. I'd been doing it all my life, and I probably would have done it that night, too, except that I had one thing to keep me from it, and that was the stack of Breville's letters in my nightstand. I knew that if I came home alone and was lonely, I could stay up and write to Breville about how I felt, and in a few days I'd get an answer back. I would always get an answer back.

So if I needed another example of how Breville's words absolved me, I had it that night as I fell asleep in my tattered old nightgown after reading a hundred pages of *Bleak House* instead of lying awake all night beside a man I didn't know.

Breville's letters were my safety net.

15

THE NEXT TIME I went down to Stillwater, Breville had the trustee take another photo of us in front of the blue backdrop with our arms draped loosely around each other's waist. It was a nicer photo than the one on the day of our first visit—my eyes were partly closed in that snapshot—and I wanted Breville to keep it. But he insisted I take it.

"I don't have another thing I can give you, Suzanne," he said, there in front of the burly, Polaroid-toting trustee. "Please just take it."

"All right, then," I said. "This one's mine."

When I got home I studied the photo, and no matter how I tried to remember it was a picture of Breville and me in front of a wall at Stillwater state prison, that detail would not stay in my mind. We looked like any other new couple. Nervous, perhaps, arms lightly looped around each other, neither of us sure we should hold the other closer. But exactly like any other young couple. Where I was blond, Breville was dark-haired, but that seemed to make us complement each other. Although I thought Breville was the better-looking of the two of us, the picture flattered me, too. It showed my long hair spilling over one shoulder, and there was something lively in my face that I couldn't quite put my finger on. It was there in

Breville's face, too. And that's how the next stage started, with me writing about what I saw in the photo and cautiously trying to describe my attraction to him.

"Your face pleases me in a way I wasn't expecting," I wrote that night back at the cabin with the Polaroid in front of me. "But more than that, I like how your expression changes over the course of time we spend in the visiting room. Your look grows softer as we sit together, as does your voice. Maybe that is why this second photo is better than the first: because you have become more yourself around me."

Breville wrote in his letter back to me:

Wow, you flatter me. I don't know how to even respond to the things you say. I don't think anyone has ever seen me the way you do. It makes me happy in a way I can't describe. As for you, I don't understand why you have ever had a moment's doubt about your looks. From how you described yourself in your letters, I was expecting someone who was plainer, homely even, to be honest. But you are a looker, a beauty, and a natural beauty, at that. I hate it when women wear too much makeup. I hate to see it caked up on their skin. Your beauty is genuine. It all just adds to my impression of you.

Things might have remained there and innocent enough, but I pushed things further along in my next letter. I want to be clear about that: I was the one who pressed on, not Breville. I knew I was opening a door, but I wanted to open it—or maybe I just couldn't stop myself from opening it.

"I like to kiss," I wrote. "And I like kisses that are a combination of hard and soft. When I kiss a man, I start out by keeping my hand by his mouth, and I touch his lips with my fingers as I kiss him. I make him keep his eyes open and sometimes I keep mine open. I start and stop kissing him many times. It takes a long time before I touch his lips with my tongue, and when I do, the touch is light. Not that I don't like deep kisses, too. But there's a time for them, and I want to build up to it."

By writing that way, I told myself, I wanted to be honest about who I was, emotionally and sexually, but of course I knew it was more than that. I wanted to excite Breville.

This was what Breville wrote back:

> Suanne, Suzanne. The way you describe a kiss is the best thing I think I have ever read. I've read your letter about fifty times now, and each time I read that paragraph, it sends shivers through me as much as it did the first time I read it. I don't know if anyone has ever kissed me the way you describe. Maybe I was just too impatient to let a woman kiss me that way. I can see that now, but I don't think I could have understood it at eighteen or nineteen. I thought I was in charge of everything. Now I can see how stupid I was, just another of the many ways.

When I read that, it took a moment to sink in that Breville was not talking about things that happened three months ago, or six, or even a year ago. He was writing about the way he used to kiss when he was still a teenager because that's how old he'd been when he was incarcerated. He'd told me inmates and visitors used to be allowed to kiss on the lips in front of the visiting room guards, but even those kisses would have been quick pecks. So Breville had gone seven years without really kissing a woman. When I stopped and thought about that, I felt chagrin at having raised the issue, and I could only wonder at the sorrow Breville must have felt, no matter what else my words provoked.

"How do you stand it?" I wrote in my next letter to him. "How do you stand not being able to kiss or touch? What do you do with your sexuality?" I thought for a while before I wrote the next sentence because I didn't know if I wanted to ask the question or get the answer. But then I thought, *No, Suzanne, you have to ask.* So I wrote, "Have you found any kind of homosexual release? I can understand if you would have."

Breville wrote:

I was wondering when that would come up. It's okay, though, I know it has to. You ask how I stand not being able to touch anyone. Well, it is impossible to stand. You can't stand it or, at least I can't, so I bury it. I bury it and I bury it. And once every couple of weeks I have a date with Rosie. That's a prison joke that you probably won't get—Rosie is my right hand. Ha, I thought I might as well tell you. I put a towel over a certain portion of my door for ten or fifteen minutes and I masturbate. We are allowed some magazines in here, and I sometimes use those. As far as the rest—I know some people turn to homosexuality in here. In certain parts of the prison at certain times, that's all there is. The inmates are like animals. All you can hear is guys yelling, "Wump, there it is." That probably makes you sick—I know it does me. It's one of the reasons I worked so hard to get on this wing, the good-behavior wing. One of my closest friends here is gay and has AIDS—Gates. You'll probably see him sometime in the visiting room. I don't hold it against him, and he is the truest friend I have here. But as for me, it holds no interest. I don't have one homosexual bone in my body. I don't mind answering any questions you have, but if it's all the same to you, I'd rather hear about your sweet kisses than think about the options I have in here with the faithful Rosie. I hope you don't mind that I try to make a joke about it, otherwise it's too depressing.

I didn't have any experience with most of the things Breville described, and yet his words made me wonder. If he was friends with

Gates, it would seem he had some open-mindedness about homosexuality, and if that was true, why would he deny himself that option, especially under the circumstances imposed by Stillwater? Maybe I had it wrong, but I also got the feeling that Breville was telling me what he believed I wanted to hear, the way he did when he wrote me his first letters and told me about his 12-step program. But if what he said about his sex life in prison raised doubts in my mind about his honesty or actual experiences, all the better. I knew he was damaged, and I also knew whatever kind of friendship I was forming with him was a reflection of my own damage. But it was all up front. I didn't have any illusions about what I was getting into.

I couldn't claim that about any number of men I had dated in the past. I hadn't really known my college boyfriend Phillip, who decided when he was seeing me that, in fact, he was bisexual; one morning he let himself into my dorm room and climbed into bed with me, cooing about the "difference" between my skin and that of the man he'd just spent the night with. I hadn't known the South African with whom I'd found such sexual bliss but who then claimed ancestral spirits were warning him against me, or the crazy Russian émigré who struck me in the breasts after he woke from a terrible dream, or the amorous young lawyer who got my telephone number one night at a club but who turned out to be terrified of me on our subsequent date—apparently because he realized in his sobriety I had bigger tits and hips than he remembered or believed he was attracted to.

And not Richaux. I certainly had not known what I was getting into with Richaux, who was the main reason I had to come north this summer. Last year he bewitched me with his stories of vision quests and his scars from sun dances, but over the winter he'd turned bullying and mean, withholding everything from me, including his tongue in my vagina. In the end, though, I left him, not for something he did, but for something he almost did.

With Breville there would be no nasty surprises, and if there were, all I had to do was stop showing up at Stillwater state prison, where Breville would be safely locked away for another seven years. There was always that safety catch in the back of my mind.

Yet if there quickly came to be something sexual between Breville and me, something entirely different began to develop, too. It showed itself in the visiting room the last time I'd seen him, the day we took the good photo. It was getting close to the time I knew the guards would call the end of the visit, and neither Breville nor I could think of anything to say to fill the time. The silence wasn't embarrassing or uncomfortable, though—we were some-how just content to sit there in the chairs, looking across the aisle at each other.

"Do you know what song I think of when I think of your name?" he asked me lazily, as if we were someplace altogether different, just passing the time together.

"What, are you going to tell me I take you down to the river?" I said, meaning to tease. "Or that you want me to give you Chinese tea and oranges?"

"No, no. But you'll probably laugh anyway. I shouldn't even tell you."

"Now you have to tell me."

"All right. I think of that old song, 'Goodnight, Irene.'"

"'Goodnight, Irene'?"

"It's an old-fashioned song, but you make me think of it. Your name is old-fashioned."

"It's a pretty song," I said. "It wouldn't be old-fashioned if someone modern sang it."

"I change the words to it anyway. Instead of 'Goodnight, Irene,' it's 'Goodnight, Suzanne.' It's 'Goodnight, Suzanne, goodnight, Suzanne, I'll hold you when I can.'"

There in the visiting room at Stillwater, with the other inmates and their visitors sitting not far from us, with the guards monitoring everything, Breville quietly half sang and half spoke the words to me.

"I do hold you when I can. I hold you here," he said then, and touched one finger to his forehead.

I didn't know what to say or do. I was so taken aback I couldn't think. So I said, "I'm moved. I mean, that you think of me that way."

"Always."

When we embraced in front of the guard's station that day, Breville held me as long as he could and whispered into my hair, *Goodnight, Suzanne.* And even though it was daytime when I left the prison, I felt like it should have been night, all because of that song.

16

RICHAUX DID A DOZEN THINGS I should have left him for, but as I said, I left him for something he did not do. Or, to be clearer, for something he almost did.

He had no idea who he would buy from this particular day. His regular dealer was out of town, but he figured if he drove around he'd see someone who looked likely. I shouldn't make it seem like he was alone—I was there in the car. But it was his weed and his high we were seeking. I was happy enough with the vodka I had at home.

We turned one corner and a bunch of people were standing outside a house on that warm May day. Richaux kept peering out the window at the people—it was his old neighborhood and he thought he might know someone. He should have stopped the car if he was going to look as long and hard as he did, but that would have been against all the rules of our covert, dope-seeking mission. He never saw the girl running out into the street.

I realized we would hit her as the front of the car came nearer to the place she would be. What's it called—trajectory? The place where the girl would be if she kept running. And she did keep running because she didn't see him or the car. She didn't even look. She was a kid playing a game, running after a friend.

I screamed Richaux's name. Without looking or thinking, he slammed on the brakes and we both lurched forward. My face came close to the glass and what I saw was this:

The girl never stopped running. She put one hand on the hood of the car and pushed it away. That's what it looked like. I saw a bare arm ending in a left hand, and the hand pushing off the corner of the car, right above where the headlight would be. The hand and arm pushed off, and the haunch of the girl's leg followed. For just a second she looked toward us, through the windshield and into the car. Then she kept running, in front of the now-motionless car. My car.

After the girl's arm and haunch and the side of her face disappeared, I turned to look at Richaux. He looked surprised.

"I just heard you and slammed on the brakes."

"Jesus Christ, didn't you even see her? Were you even looking?"

"I just told you," he said. "And for Christ's sake, don't be depressed. Be happy."

"Be happy?"

"Be happy I didn't hit her. It could have been a tragedy and it wasn't."

"You're a fucking tragedy," I said. I should have also said, *And I am a fucking tragedy because I'm here with you*, but I didn't. Yet it was how I felt.

We kept driving down the block and I looked back to see if any of the adults had stepped out into the street to watch us, to catch a license plate number. But no one had. It had all happened so fast no one from the group of people standing outside the house seemed to understand how close we'd come to hitting the girl. It seemed no one else saw the girl reach out and push the car away.

We continued down that street and the next and the next, and Richaux eventually found someone to buy his dope from. We came back to my place and as he smoked and I drank, Richaux berated me just to draw attention away from himself. I didn't care. It was like he wasn't even speaking to me. I knew I should have left him before—after the time he shoved his foot between my legs instead of using his hand or mouth to help me come, for instance—but I'd kept waiting for things to get better, or for a new phase to start. But the day we almost hit the girl in my car, trying to buy his dope, well, that was the day I decided to quit. Whatever else I'd done in my life, I tried to limit the effect of my actions and the chances I took. If I was careless, I tried to be careless only with my own life.

Richaux called many times after that, but I always let the phone ring. And before he could figure out that I really meant it, I was gone. I parceled out my things to Julian and Kate for the summer, and I planned to parcel myself out in September when school started again, until I found a new place to live. The truth was, apart from the externals like disconnecting the phone, it was the easiest thing in the world to leave Richaux. His stories had grown old a long time ago, and I was sick of his bullshit and bored by his dick.

In that sense I didn't need the summer so much to heal as I needed it to gather strength and move on, like a summer thunderstorm. And it had been my plan to spend my vacation alone, sorting through things, figuring out what it was I really wanted in my life, like my friend Kate said I needed to. She was the one who actually came out and said, "I want so see you with a marriage and a mortgage around your neck." As crude as it was, I understood what she was saying—she wanted to see me with something real. And to a degree I knew she was right. Sometimes everything about how I lived seemed to be some kind of half-life.

But my resolve to spend the summer on my own, contemplating and reflecting—well, that seemed to have shifted, and whatever it was I was doing with Breville, I knew he certainly did not fall into

Kate's category of worthwhile men who might have something to offer me as a partner in life. Nevertheless, I kept telling myself, I had extricated myself from the situation with Richaux, and if the only way I knew how to do it was by disappearing entirely from my old life, so be it. I had gotten the job done, and now my life was my own again. Only I could determine what I wanted it to be.

17

AFTER BREVILLE AND I started writing more intimate letters, I bought a new dress to wear when I went to see him. It was long—the guards wouldn't let you into the visiting room if your skirt was too short—but it was red, and it had a keyhole neckline.

That neckline was something. The dress had a little band-collar that buttoned at my throat, but from the base of the collar, down over my breastbone to where the line between my breasts showed—that was all open. The oval opening wasn't even that big, but because it was surrounded by fabric, it gave the feeling of something being bared.

Breville liked the dress. He told me as soon as we sat down in the chairs.

"Holy, Suzanne. How much did it cost?"

"Sixty bucks," I said.

He made a small whistle and sat shaking his head at me. I didn't want to tell him that sixty dollars was nothing for a dress, that the Paris perfume I was wearing cost more than that, or that if I'd wanted a nice dress instead of a trashy acetate one I'd have to spend much more.

"I'm glad you like it," I said instead, and I sat across from him and let him take it all in, from the keyhole neckline down to my gold shoes.

That day we sat talking about the different cities we had seen or lived in, but really, we watched each other the entire time.

"I liked New York while I lived there," I told him. "But when I left I was ready to leave."

"The one time I was there I got lost," Breville said. "I took a train somewhere and it went the wrong way. I walked back to Port Authority."

"How far did you walk?"

"A few miles. I was carrying a suitcase, too, so I was sweating like a pig."

"How old were you?"

"Eighteen. Our senior trip."

I told him a story about my father, about the time he had applied for a job after he got out of the service after the Korean War. The job advertisement had said there would be a typing test, and so my father had lugged his own typewriter to the interview, not realizing until he arrived at the office that the company would provide its own typewriters for the test.

"His arms were so tired from carrying his typewriter he couldn't take the test," I said.

Breville laughed a long time at that, and when he was done laughing, he slouched down in his chair and stretched his legs out on either side of my gold shoes. I could feel him all around me, and I could feel how, even though we were talking and laughing and enjoying each other's company, there was another level to what was going on that had nothing to do with our stories, but rather to do with watching each other and the keyhole neckline and Breville's legs stretched out on either side of mine.

"Did he ever get the job? Your dad?"

"He went back the next day and took the test," I said. "I don't remember if he got the job or not."

"You should ask him," Breville said. "Ask him and tell me."

There was nothing intimate in what we were saying to each other, nothing intimate at all—and yet everything between us had that feeling. Everything. It didn't matter if I was talking about my dad, or about how I used to like to lie on the roof and look up at the pink Brooklyn sky—every detail was personal, charged. I can't explain it. Yet even though I knew something was happening between Breville and me that day in the visiting room, and that everything we said that day was itself as well as more than itself and other than itself, it wasn't until we were saying goodbye that I understood how much had been traded back and forth between us. The guard monitoring our bodily contact for illicit exchanges could watch for a packet being passed from hand or mouth to shirt collar, but there was no way to monitor the real exchange that happened when Breville and I touched that day.

After I kissed Breville's cheek and he kissed mine, we stood holding each other in front of the guard for the few seconds permitted. As we pulled away from each other, Breville traced his hand—the one the guard could not see because our bodies blocked it—down the small of my back and over my ass and along the outside of my hip. The whole thing probably took only two or three seconds, but it seemed much longer as it was happening. I felt the weight of Breville's hand against my skin, but I also felt the heat of his hand. The thing seemed to burn, and the places where he touched me seemed to burn.

It was only my imagination, but the burning went on even after I exited the huge front doors of the prison, and as I slowly walked the leaf-filled blocks to my car. Certainly the risk was real: Breville could be sent to the hole for the wrong kind of touch in the visiting room, taken off the good-behavior wing where he had his own cell, a TV, and a morsel of control.

The burning sensation stayed with me as I got into my car and for a good many miles of my drive back north. And if it was laughable when I said that Breville did not seem like a rapist, this next statement will be laughable, too: that day was the first time I knew Breville could hurt me.

18

WHEN I FINALLY TOLD JULIAN I was driving four hours back to the Cities every week to go to Stillwater, he told me I was crazy.

"I thought you went up to that cabin to get away from this," Julian said the day I stopped by after visiting Breville. The way he waved his hand as he said "this" took in the sound of the traffic drifting in the window as well as the glass of bourbon he had in his hand. And he was right: when I left on the last day of school, I broke my lease, disconnected the phone, and left no forwarding address or number. As much as I could, I disappeared.

"I did want to get away," I said. "But visiting here is not the same as living here."

"And now you're involved with a convict," Julian said. "Why do you always have such a taste for shit?"

"I'm working through something," I told him. And there was nothing he could say to that.

Still, I knew better than to say anything about the Paris perfume, or the keyhole dress, or the sexually explicit letters I'd begun writing Breville. There would have been no way to explain those things to people, or to explain that it was exactly because Alpha Breville was a rapist that I was interested in him. He'd helped me understand my own rape, and there seemed to be some kind of symmetry to the attraction. At first it seemed perverse, and then it became more and more logical. Who better than Breville to understand me?

Usually I did the drive to and from Stillwater in a day. It meant eight hours in the car, but it was hard to mix my visits to Breville with anything that had once been my life in the Cities. One Friday, though, Julian persuaded me to stay overnight in Minneapolis; he was seeing someone new, and I could have free run of his house as long as I spent some time with his needy cat.

As I was leaving the prison that day, I gave Breville Julian's number so we could talk after our visit. And since each call could only last ten minutes on the prison phone system, Breville called me over and over. During the third call—a luxury we never had when he was calling long-distance and I had to pay the exorbitant collect rates the prison phone system charged—Breville told me he wanted to ask me something and that he'd been wanting to ask for a long time.

"Shoot," I said.

"If I call back, could I hear you, Suzanne? Can you do it so I can hear?"

I thought for a second of how every prison call was recorded, and how it was Julian's number that would be on the record, and then I thought about my last letter to Breville in which I'd written, "I bought my first vibrator when I was twenty-one, right before I moved. It's a hundred times easier than using my hand. My favorite way to masturbate is to lie perfectly still. With just the ball of my vibrator humming on my body, I force myself to relax. I try to take as long as I can, relaxing my muscles for as long as I can. When I can't hold off any longer, when I finally do let myself come, my entire body spasms because the orgasm is so strong." Was I really at all surprised when he asked if he could hear me come?

"Let me at least get myself ready," I said.

"Sure, sure," Breville said. "I'll call you back in five. Or do you need longer?"

"Just a little longer," I said.

After I hung up the phone, I went and got a pillow from the sofa. I didn't want to masturbate in Julian's bed—that seemed unforgivable, and somehow beyond the line I was willing to cross—so I took off my pants and lay down on Julian's floor. The cat kept circling around me. When Breville called back, my fingers were already wet.

"I didn't think I'd get to hear that for a long time," Breville said when I was done.

His voice was husky, and he sounded softer than I had ever heard him sound. It all made me think of how he'd spent the last seven years.

"Don't say I never did nothing for you," I told him.

"Didn't you do it for you, too?"

I didn't have the heart to tell Breville it was fake. I hadn't meant to fake—I had been masturbating, but I just couldn't come on the hard floor, holding the phone to my head, and hearing the cat walk around me. It was too much pressure. The act was ridiculous and felt hollow to me, like something out of a bad movie, but I'd still wanted to do it for Breville. Something in me wanted to do it, even if it was pretend.

"Sure," I said. "I always look out for myself."

I never told Julian what I had done. I just added it to my list of exclusions and lies.

19

BECAUSE I DIDN'T WANT to get too caught up in Breville, or perhaps because it was summer and I had time to dally with whomever I wanted, I placed another personal ad, this one in the Bemidji paper. I could have picked up someone at the Royal or some other local bar if that's all I was looking for, but it wasn't. I wanted something more than just a drunken fuck, and I thought that a person paying to answer an ad would have at least that much invested.

A cowboy visiting friends in Blackduck answered, and I called him at the number he left. We seemed to have little in common, though. After he told me the story of how a horse had kicked him in the knee at the Cody rodeo—bad enough to put him on crutches—we had trouble just keeping the conversation going. But when I tried to get off the phone, he said, "Now, don't go and hang up yet. You're like E. F. Hutton. You talk and I'll listen."

He was making an effort, it seemed, so I decided to give him a chance, and when I showed up at the appointed time at the Paul Bunyan statue in Bemidji, right beneath the horns of Babe, I was glad I hadn't been put off by his manner. The cowboy stood six-five, with blue eyes and jet hair. His shoulders were broad and his hips were narrow, and not even his crutches or hobbling could take away from his handsomeness.

"So, you weren't kidding about your knee," I said in those first flustered seconds after shaking his hand, when I was still taking in the good-looking whole of him. "Are you seeing a doctor?"

"I've been doctoring myself," he told me. "Ibuprofen and beer."

We sat by the water and again he told me the story of the horse kicking him in Cody. After that, he confessed to me that he was nervous about the date.

"I had a few beers before I came here," he said. "Liquid courage."

"Would you like to go have a drink now?"

"No, no," he said. "I had them at home. It's cheaper than drinking in a bar."

And of course that told me a couple of things, but I didn't let any of it register in my face.

When some teenage boys walked by, laughing and talking loudly, I looked away from the cowboy for just a second and drew my purse a little closer to my side.

"You don't need to worry about that as long as I'm here," the cowboy said. "I don't let anyone bother a woman, even if I am on crutches."

We sat talking about his trip out here, and he told me about the dog he lost in Cody after the rodeo. He had the dog so well trained it didn't need a leash, and when he'd gone into a bar, he felt safe leaving the dog in the back of his pickup.

"If he left, it's because someone took him," the cowboy said. "He'd never leave on his own. When I bought steak, I'd buy one for him and one for me."

"Did you look for him?"

"I gave up after a day."

"Do you remember the name of the bar where you were? You could call."

"I remember," the cowboy said, looking out over Lake Bemidji. "I should. I should call."

"What was your dog's name?"

"Bear. But I called him Bud Dog for short."

I didn't say that Bud Dog was longer than Bear. I knew what the cowboy was saying, and I knew he missed the dog.

I guess we'd talked long enough then, or long enough for the cowboy to decide he liked me, because he looked back at me then and invited me up to his friends' house in Blackduck.

"Bob and Thrace can grill us up some steaks," he said, so politely and gravely I knew I wasn't supposed to take him up on the offer.

"If you like, we could drive back to my place and I could fix us some dinner," I said, though I knew I had next to nothing in the house and was no cook, even on my best days.

"Well, that sounds nice, too," the cowboy told me. He was measured as he said it, so maybe the relief I thought I heard in his voice was all in my imagination. But that's what I felt—relief over not having to meet his friends and gain their approval as well as his.

We made the long drive back to my cabin, with the cowboy following me in his old blue pickup. When we stopped along the way to get beer in Emmaville, I walked over to his vehicle before I went into the store. "So, are you sure you like me well enough to come all this way?" I asked.

"I wouldn't be here if I didn't like you. Do you need me to lick your fingers?"

He sounded petulant and I didn't know what I'd done to break the bantering mood we'd established by the lake, but I chalked it up to whatever pain his knee was causing him. When I pulled out of the parking lot of the Emmaville General Store, the cowboy again fell in line behind me.

By the time we got to the cabin, it seemed he had lost his impatience.

"I guess you only date guys who are as tall as you are," he teased when we got to the low-hanging branches of the jack pine by the cabin door. At five-four, I had no trouble scooting under the limbs, but the cowboy not only had to duck but also bend at the knee. On crutches and one good leg, it was awkward.

Inside and seated, though, with a beer in hand, he again became handsome and charming, telling me one story after another. He was named after an archangel by his Jehovah's Witness parents, whom he'd run away from when he was thirteen. He once swallowed a bullet on a barroom dare. Another time, to prove a point, he jumped in the Kern River with his boots on and fully clothed. Just a couple weeks ago he stitched up his own leg with needle and thread when he got cut in the woods, helping his Blackduck friend with some logging.

"And once I put my finger through someone's windpipe because he was hurting someone," the cowboy said. He then told me the story about hearing a woman screaming for help in the parking lot when he lived in Denver. A man was assaulting her and the cowboy pulled the guy off. Since the cowboy didn't have any kind of weapon with him, he punched the attacker in the face and then punctured the guy's windpipe with his finger.

"I told you I don't allow anyone to hurt a woman," he said.

I let the cowboy go on talking because he seemed to need it, and because my stories about working with teenagers and grading papers paled beside his tales.

"Do you think you could fix me something to eat now?" he asked me after his second beer. "That's how my last girlfriend got me. She promised me three squares a day."

I didn't know if spaghetti and leftover chicken constituted a square meal, but that was what I had in the house, so that was what I made the cowboy. He went through three helpings, along with four slices of bread. If I'd made more food, he would have eaten it, but there was no more. For dessert, I put half a pack of cookies on a plate and the cowboy ate all but the one I took to keep him company.

"I gave my last four hundred dollars to my friends," the cowboy told me then. "I've been staying with them, and they've been feeding me. And Monday I have a doctor's appointment."

And that's when I knew precisely where things stood with him.

After dinner the cowboy hobbled down to the dock with me and watched me swim, and then we came back to the cabin and he went through my video collection to find something for us to watch. He picked out a PBS documentary about the West that I was previewing for my American literature class. At one point when some scholar was talking about Crazy Horse, the cowboy leaned close and kissed me, as I'd been hoping he might. But the thing went no further, not even when I said, "Hmm, that was good."

"It was just chicken scratch," he said, and we went on watching the documentary.

It wasn't until the video was over and the cowboy said, "Well, I guess I should be going," that I realized there was a formula I was supposed to follow, a series of offers to be made and rejected, then revised and accepted.

"It's awfully late," I said, and it was—nearly two a.m. "You can stay here if you like."

"I can sleep on the sofa."

"You can sleep in the bed with me if you want," I said, and then I quickly went into the bathroom to brush my teeth so he could have a second to mull it over.

That must have been how long it took him to decide, too, because by the time I came back from the bathroom, he was stripped down to his underwear and lying on the bed. When I saw him, I felt the same thing I always felt when I was about to lie down with a stranger—I loved the directness of it, the intention. I felt it even more strongly when I saw the cowboy's body. His bare chest and the dark hair on his thighs made me want to lie down with him. But something about him—knowing he had a bum knee, or even the full white briefs he was wearing that made him look old-fashioned—something about him made me wonder if he didn't need a soft place to fall more than he needed a lay.

It was only after we were lying in my bed—him in his white underwear and me in a cotton nightgown with my eyes closed, trying to pretend I was going to sleep—that he revealed the next part of the formula.

"Are you attracted to me?" the cowboy said into the dark room. He sounded unsure—unsteady, even—and I thought about what he might feel like, lying there in the rough cabin with his crutches beside the bed. He wasn't whole, but whatever it was that had driven him to seek out company must have been stronger than whatever pain he was in.

"I am attracted to you," I said.

It was all I had to do. The cowboy rolled over from lying on his back and pulled himself on top of me. After a couple minutes of kissing and rubbing at my breasts, he lifted himself with his good leg and worked his way inside of me. Because he couldn't hold his weight evenly, he lay heavily on me. I told myself that was why I felt a kind of panic, but it was more than that. He was a foot taller than I was, and strong, even with his bad leg, and even though I'd felt such desire for him all evening, once he got inside me, the plainness of the act struck me. It felt rushed and wrong.

When the cowboy came after just a little while, he shook his head from side to side, like he was seizuring. Then he made a sound I'd never heard a man make before. It was a cross between a whine and a howl, like a coyote or a dog. The whole thing scared me, and I felt some kind of shiver at the back of my neck and over my scalp, but I told myself, *That's just the way he is, that's just his way.* And in a second or two, even though the sound scared me, I wanted it, too. Wanted him to be an animal.

After it was over, he rolled off me but kept one hand wrapped in my hair. I still felt the shivery thing over my scalp, but I also felt bound to him, to the naked thing he'd shown me.

"You've got me here now," the cowboy said then. "What are you going to do with me?"

At first I thought it was some of the same bad temper I'd heard when we'd stopped in Emmaville, but when I looked at him in the dark—there was enough moonlight coming in the window that I could see his face clearly—I saw it wasn't that at all. So I climbed over his bad leg, spread his thighs, and took his cock in my mouth. Then there was nothing he could say.

The second time we screwed, I sat on top of the cowboy. The ceiling of the cabin was so low that once I straddled him, I could touch it. Not just touch it—I could press my palms flat against it. I did it a few times, so he could see my breasts go high and so I could have something to brace myself against as I fucked him. It was better that way than the first time when he'd been on top.

"Am I hurting you?" I asked, thinking of his bum knee and the crutches beside the bed.

"You hurt me good. Grind away."

I did it hard enough that he moved up on the bed a little with each push. That kind of screwing didn't make me feel much of anything, but I liked seeing him move like that.

When he came, he shook his head again and made the same sound he had the first time. I was ready for it this time.

When I got up in the middle of the night to walk down to the dock to swim, the cowboy didn't wake or even shift on the bed. I knew it was the beer and the fucking that made him sleep so hard, but it made me marvel. Now that I had fucked him, he stayed fucked, asleep and entirely trusting, even though I was a stranger to him. I could have gone through his wallet or gone out to the kitchen to get a knife. Yet I didn't want a knife, and I knew he didn't have any money. I didn't even want to check his driver's license to see if he had told me his real name.

The next morning, when we woke up, I gave the cowboy a blow job. I kept the head of his penis in my mouth and worked my lips and hand over the shaft of his cock until he came. When he was done seizing and howling, he said, "No one ever done me like that before."

I didn't know if he meant he never got to come in a woman's mouth before, or if my combination of hand and blow job was unique. I thought I might ask, but as we were lying there, sweetly, the cowboy lightly fingered the notches in my throat.

"See, you can go in with your finger, right between the ridges," he said.

I could have knocked his hand away or told him he was scaring me, but I did neither. Instead I went still like an animal and in a little while he moved his hand away from my throat.

We had sex a couple more times that morning, and then I made us coffee, eggs, and home fries. When the cowboy tried my coffee, he told me it was too strong.

"It's good for another kind of a day, when you want to get something done," he said. "Another day I'll sit here on your sofa and read the paper and you can make me that kind of coffee."

So I poured myself a cup, threw the rest out, and started a new pot for him.

When the cowboy and I sat down to eat, I told him how I'd found the cabin to rent.

"I don't miss anything about the things I left behind," I said. "I wish I could just stay here."

"Why don't you?"

"It's a summer cabin. I couldn't make it through the winter here. And I have a job to go back to in September."

"If you like it, you should stay. You'd find a way. At least you have a place you want to be."

"Why, where would you like to be? Where's home for you?"

"Always the questions!" the cowboy said, laughing, leaning back in an old wooden chair until it tipped back on two legs. "I haven't had a home since I was thirteen. That's when I went to work with my uncle. And that's when I became 'as one dead' to my family. Did you ever hear of that?"

"Is it a religious thing?"

"It's what you do to someone who doesn't believe in Jehovah, even if it's your own son."

I was going to ask if it was like shunning, which I'd heard about, but then I looked at the cowboy's face. He seemed deeply troubled— angry and agitated. It happened in an instant, too, just the way it had seemed to happen the night before when his mood went from teasing to impatient right before my eyes. So I didn't say anything. I just sat, listening and watching. Picking quietly at my eggs.

"My own mother and father," he said after a while. "I've been on my own ever since. To them I don't exist."

"So that can't be your home."

"No can do."

"Well, maybe the thing to do is pick a place where you're happy," I said. "Pick a place and say, 'This is it.'"

"Do you think?" the cowboy asked.

At first I thought he was making fun of me for trying to make it all sound so simple. You know, that I thought he could just pick a place and it would make everything all right. But I looked at his face and I saw he wasn't making fun of me at all. He was asking me, genuinely.

"Yes," I said. "I think maybe the thing to do is decide to try to be happy."

"Do you think I could make a living down where you live?"

"In the Cities? It depends what kind of work you do."

"Heating and air-conditioning. I've been in it for fifteen years."

"I don't see why not. There's plenty of people down there. Plenty of businesses."

"Could I move in with you?"

"Do you want to move in with me?"

"Would you have me?"

"Sure," I said. "Sure. I'd love to have you."

It was out of my mouth before I could stop it. But after I said it, I realized I meant it. Just as I had felt myself open up to him the night before when he shuddered and howled, it now seemed like something inside of me was breaking open again.

He nodded then, but we didn't talk about it anymore—we just went back to bed and he *ki-yi* yowled for me again.

When the cowboy said goodbye that afternoon—after we called out to the Silver Dollar in Cody to see if anyone had found Bud Dog, after he took a shower and gave me a narration of his scars, after I marveled again at the smoothness of his skin and the exact quality of softness and hardness I felt in his arms, after he let me help him with his leg brace—he told me he'd call me the next day when he got back from his doctor's appointment.

"We'll make some plans," he said.

"All right," I said. "All right, then." And I gave him the rest of the cookies for the trip back to Blackduck.

The rest of that day and the next morning, I thought of him, sketching out our life back in Minneapolis. I thought daydreamily about the way things could be, but I also made myself think about what I'd be taking on with him, with his moodiness and seeming destitution. They were warning signs, I knew—I knew that. But difficult people were capable and deserving of love—I knew that, too. And none of it mattered anyway, because for whatever odd set of reasons or pheromones, I'd already fallen in love with the cowboy. I'd already decided to open my life to him.

20

BUT THE COWBOY NEVER CALLED. Not the day he said he would, or the day after, or the day after that. When I finally broke down at the end of the week and called the Blackduck number he'd left when he answered the ad, I only reached his friends.

"He's gone back to Wyoming," the wife told me. "He had some business to settle there."

When she said that, I thought of the conversation Julian and I had had a long time ago, when we were just becoming friends.

"I always think it's love," I'd told him. "I always think sex will be a mainline to the heart."

"You mean every time you screw, you think you'll fall in love?"

"I'm usually a bit in love already," I said. "It's stupid, I know."

"It's not stupid," Julian said. "It's just a fucking tragic flaw."

It was impossible to explain to him in his world-weariness what I meant, what I believed in my heart, what I still believed. It wasn't that I thought every lay was love, and there was a part of me that doubted everything about the cowboy. Even as I was bewitched by him, I'd wondered at some of the things he'd said, which seemed like lines from some Merle Haggard song.

But without some belief on my part, without some spirit of

generosity, there was no point in bothering with any of it. No point in stripping down, in spreading my legs, in opening myself. At the moment I picked a man, he was not troubled, not rough traffic, not just the embodiment of animal magnetism and sexual attraction. At the moment I picked a man, he held all possibility, all eloquent potential. And if only he could turn out to be what he promised to be at the outset, he would be—could be—a great love. That was the river I kept going to, drinking from. It didn't matter if the cowboy was what he said he was or not. Something in me liked something in him. If he had frightened me the first time he fucked me, he had also opened me up. I don't know how else to say it.

"Tell Brill I asked about him," I said to the wife. "When you speak to him again, tell him I wish him the best."

And I hung up the phone.

21

I DIDN'T WANT TO CALL JULIAN with the story of my latest failure in love—as appropriate as his lecture would have been, I still didn't want to hear it. But I felt fragile and distracted, so I started a letter to Breville. He was someone faithful to return to, if only on paper.

"Sometimes it seems my life has been shaped by my rape—the entire last seventeen years," I wrote to Breville. "If I had to say one thing that has been the most damaging, it has been constantly seeing myself in the light of that night. Constantly wondering what I might have been like if it hadn't happened. Would I be able to be friends with men instead of just fucking them? Would I see them and myself differently? Would I see my vagina differently? My pussy? My cunt?"

I threw the letter away. It made me seem like too much of a victim. And instead of writing to Breville at all, I got in the car and drove down to Stillwater to see him. I told myself the drive would do me good, get me out of the space I was in, but of course it wasn't just that. I wanted to see Breville just like I would any friend.

I'd never shown up like that, unannounced, and I waited a long time before the guards called, "Visit for Breville." And when I got into the visiting room, to the taped-off square, I could see the concern on Breville's face before he embraced me.

"What's wrong?" he said as he held me. "Did something happen?"

"Nothing happened," I said.

When we got to a couple of chairs—not our usual spot, because it was late in the day, and the visiting room was crowded—Breville asked me again if something was wrong.

"Really, nothing's wrong," I said. "It's just been a hard week. I needed to get away."

I could see I'd alarmed him, so I made myself sit back. He kept watching me, and I let him. I watched him, too. He looked different than he had other days. His hair was neat, but I could see he hadn't showered or shaved that day, and he was wearing a dark green T-shirt, jogging pants, and prison-issue canvas shoes.

"You caught me off guard," he said when he saw me looking. "I was actually cooking dinner."

"You get to cook?"

"We make things on our wing," he said. "We have a microwave and put together stuff from the commissary. Prison cuisine."

"I probably shouldn't have dropped in on you."

"Don't say that," Breville told me. "I'm glad to see you. But what happened?"

"Life," I said. "Just life."

He seemed to relax a little the longer I sat there, but I could see he still wondered what it was all about. And I think on some level he must have known, because after about fifteen minutes of small talk he said to me, "You don't have to do my time with me, Suzanne."

"What do you mean?"

"You don't need to do my time with me. You need to live your life."

"I am living my life."

"Are you?"

"I am," I said. "Living my life. Believe me."

He looked at me for a long time when I said that. Neither one of us said anything then.

In a little while a voice came over the loudspeaker, saying, "Breville, five minutes."

I'd been there for less than an hour, not my usual two.

"They limit it sometimes," Breville said. "When the room's crowded. Can I call you? Are you staying down here tonight with your friend?"

"I didn't make any plans."

"So you're driving back up there?"

"It stays light late."

"Do me a favor, then," Breville said. "I want you to call my mother. Call her and talk to her."

"Why should I call your mother?"

"She's good to talk to. You can talk to her about anything."

"I'm okay," I said. "I have friends to talk to. I just needed to go for a drive and I came down here. There's nothing to worry about."

"Then call her for me."

"For you?"

"I mean, call her for me. Do it for me. I want her to know you."

"Can I think about it?" I said. "Can you let me think about it?"

"Sure you can think about it. Of course you can."

Still, he said her number several times and asked me to repeat it twice.

"Just in case," he said.

In the taped-off square that day, Breville held me as long as he could. He ran his hands down my sides and over the small of my back and pressed me to him. I thought I could feel his cock through his pants. Maybe that was what I had driven four hours for, to feel that.

Before Breville let me go, he said into my hair, "You are sweet, you are so sweet to me."

"You are sweet to me, too," I said.

When we walked away from each other that day, we both turned and we both made the pass through the air with our hands. *Steady as she goes*, we said with our palms, pushing away the air. *Smooth. Until next time*, we said with our hands.

Until then.

I made the drive home in under four hours, stopping only once in Motley for gas. When I got back to the cabin, even though it was past ten, there was still some light in the sky. I couldn't really see it when I walked down to the lake, but once I was out in the water, I could make out the glow in the west. Dark blue, a paring of moon. The water was black, and fragrant—from what, I didn't know. Maybe it was the smell of the wildflowers and shrubs on the bank, mixing in the moist night air, but to me it seemed like the water itself was perfumed. It was like water in a dream. That's what I swam in.

I didn't go far out into the lake—a boat would never see me in that darkness—but I couldn't stand to stay close to the dock, either. I didn't want to feel anything beneath my feet. When I was out a hundred feet or so, I just stayed in place, treading water, pushing it away with my hands. It was the easiest thing. The water felt like silk on my hands. No—it felt like water.

I didn't know what to think about Breville, about how I felt about him, about how I felt more kindness from him in the taped-off square in front of the guard than I had in bed with the cowboy.

I thought about the way the cowboy's skin had felt then, and what it had been like to kiss him. Like swimming in deep water. I didn't know how a kiss could be like that, unless it was everything in the cowboy coming out, because it was clear he was dark water. There was the moodiness that kept surfacing even in the short time we'd spent together, the barroom dares and fights, the talk about his rigid parents who had disowned him when he was still a boy. And then there was the seizuring and howling he'd done when he came. I hadn't realized it at the time, but he'd sounded like the wolves I'd heard in the distance one night at the cabin.

But then I thought about lying between his legs, right before I took his cock in my mouth. I thought of the moment right before, and then when I touched him and sucked on him, finding a way to take more of him into my mouth. When I liked a man, really liked him, there was something so sweet, so lollipop-good, about sucking his cock, and that was how I'd felt about the cowboy. I kept hearing him say, *No one ever done me like that*, and I kept seeing the way his face looked when he said it.

Not that it mattered, since he was gone, but I'd felt both fear and the lollipop-good feeling with the cowboy. I couldn't make sense of the two things together, so I just turned and floated on my back and let myself think about it all. The cowboy with his smooth skin and Breville with his burning hands. I couldn't touch Breville, couldn't know him, and I'd touched the cowboy, but I didn't know him, either. They were both ciphers. That's what I lay thinking about, floating, cradled in the fragrant water of the dark lake.

22

FOR MY NEXT VISIT to Breville, I wore a black blazer with no blouse underneath. It buttoned just above my bra, and on my breastbone I wore a necklace of onyx and marcasite. Its triangular pendant pointed to the skin between my breasts that was shiny with perfume.

Breville took it all in as he was supposed to. "Nice jacket," he told me when we were seated in our plastic chairs.

"Thank you."

"Nice necklace. Wish I could wear it."

I didn't understand his words or tone, but it made me think back to the day he assured me that he didn't have a homosexual bone in his body, that no one "messed" with him. It all made me wonder about Breville, about who he really was in prison, and what details of his life he edited out for me.

As if he could read my thoughts and doubts and wanted to re-route them, Breville said, "Nice breasties." As if he were a kid.

"I wish I could suck your nipples," he then told me, quietly. And wasn't such a kid.

I had that on my mind, I think, so I asked Breville to tell me what he was like as a kid.

"What do you want to know?"

"Anything you want to tell me," I said. "What did you do for fun?"

"Chased girls and raised hell. What all boys do. What were you like?"

"Oh, I was a good kid. Shy. All anyone had to do was look at me cross and I cried."

"Tenderhearted," Breville said.

"I think so. That's what my mother tells me."

"How old were you when you lost your virginity?"

"Fifteen," I said. "When I was in the ninth grade."

"What made you wait so long?"

"I didn't think I did," I said. "Besides, I was fooling around a lot before that. Why? How old were you?"

"When I lost my virginity? Eight."

"Eight years old?"

"I couldn't come, but that was the first time I had sex. With an older girl. My cousin, as a matter of fact. She started it."

I didn't know what to say to that—it shocked me and I didn't know how to hide it. But Breville seemed to want to go on talking, so I tried to pretend it was a regular conversation.

"You could have an erection when you were eight?"

"That's how it got done," Breville said. "I think I was about a year older when I came the first time."

"That seems way too young."

"When I used to get mad at my mom, I'd just run away. Usually I'd stay away until I got laid."

"How old were you then?"

"Ten, eleven. Then, when I was about fourteen, this older lady took a shine to me. She was in her twenties or thirties. I'd stay with her long enough to get what I wanted, then I'd go through her purse when she was in the bathroom. Steal her money or her dope. Whatever I could find."

"What did she do?"

"Ahh, she got pissed off at me, of course," Breville said. He sat up as he said that, and when he leaned back in his chair again, he slouched down and stretched his legs on either side of mine.

"She'd try to kick me in the ass," he said, laughing. "But I was younger and could run faster."

After he told me that, we sat there not talking. I tried to think about what Breville had just told me, but I could barely take in the information. At eight I was in third grade and liked playing with kittens and my dollhouse. Whatever precociousness I displayed by rummaging around through my father's girlie magazines was nothing compared to Breville's early sexual experiences, and they threw a new light on his crime. When he raped that woman in South Minneapolis at nineteen, he did it after being molested at eight by his twelve-year-old cousin, and after ten or eleven years of fucking. And I finally understood the thing he'd told me the first day I came to see him: the love of his mother or grandfather could not save him from the years of underage drinking, abuse, petty thievery, and sexual escapades. By the time he was nineteen, he'd been running wild for a lifetime.

"You'll have to wear a short skirt one day," Breville told me then, jarring me out of my thoughts.

When I looked across the aisle at him, slouched down in his chair, I could see something in his eyes that was soft and glittering at the same time.

"I don't think I have a short skirt."

"Maybe you should buy one," he said. "No, that's all right. You don't have to. It doesn't matter."

He looked away from me then, but when he looked back, he shook his head.

"It doesn't matter," he told me. "I'm just happy you come see me. That you sit across from me and talk to me."

"Maybe I could unbutton a few more buttons on one of the dresses I have."

"Do you think you could?"

"Maybe," I said. "I'll see."

"Do you understand what I'm saying?"

It took me a moment to understand what he meant. But then I followed his eyes down to his jeans, and I finally understood what he was telling me.

"It's just from talking to you, Suzanne. Do you see now?"

"I understand."

For the rest of the visit, I don't know what we talked about. Nothing, really. I just sat across the aisle from Breville, between his legs, I let him sit there with his hard cock, talking to me, and when we stood inside the taped-off square, I let him push his cock against my belly for the moment we were allowed in front of the guards.

"Sweet Suzanne," he said into my hair.

I didn't have time to say anything back, but when I left the prison that day, I carried all of that—on my skin and in my hair. In me.

23

AFTER I INTRODUCED MYSELF to Jacqui Breville on the phone, she sounded surprised for only a second.

"Alpha has told me what a good friend you've been" she said. "I've heard some nice things about you."

"I'm glad to hear that."

We chatted for a moment about the weather in Rapid City, South Dakota, which was where she was living, and I told her I'd been through Kadoka a few times.

"Then you understand," she said. "All the kids cleared out of there as soon as they could. So did I."

"Small-town life isn't for everyone," I said. "I know it wasn't for me."

We chatted awhile longer—about her youngest daughter, about where my family lived, about what I did for a living and how nice it was to have summers off—and it was all so pleasant and light-hearted, I could have been talking to anyone, absolutely anyone, except the mother of a convicted rapist in Stillwater state prison. But why would it have been otherwise? To Jacqui Breville, I was a complete stranger. Even if she did want to fulfill her son's request to be friendly to me, there was no reason to discuss anything more pressing than the weather.

We kept up the patter a little longer, and then I said, "Well, I don't want to keep you. I just wanted to introduce myself and say hello."

"I'm glad you did," she said. "It was nice to talk with you."

"It was good to talk with you, too," I said.

We were so polite it was almost funny. It wasn't until I hung up that I thought about the phone call from her perspective. Her incarcerated son, whom she'd been powerless over since he was eight or nine, asked her to talk with a woman who'd been visiting him at prison. And I could only imagine what Breville told her about me. That we were writing to each other, that I came to visit every week, that I was lonely—I had no idea. But I figured Jacqui had seen it come and go, and if I were in her shoes, the question I would have wanted to ask would have been, *What do you want with my son?*

Or maybe Breville told her my story and tried to get her to understand we were somehow good for each other. And maybe he told her he was falling in love with me. Or that I was falling in love with him. I believe he could have told her any number of things—and not a single one of them would have made sense to her, or answered the question of what I wanted from her son, which was a question not even I could answer.

But a couple of things were clear to me from my short conversation. Breville's mother not only loved him, she actively supported him, at least as much as she could from another state and nine hours away. If she didn't, she never would have taken the time to have the nebulously sweet conversation with me that she'd had. And I thought that meant the world—not to me, but to Breville. His mother loved and supported him now during his incarceration, just as she had loved and supported him when he'd been a hell-raising teenager. He had told me that, and I had heard in Jacqui Breville's voice that it was true. Because in spite of how noncommittal her conversation had been with me, it had, in fact, been an act of kindness on her part to sound so pleasant and friendly to me. Whatever else had been going on in her day—and I had reason to believe from Breville that his mother did not have the easiest life—she had done what she could to assist her son in his new friendship or courtship or craziness with me.

When I realized that, it humbled me. It humbled me that on a day when I had been upset and had driven to Stillwater to add my particular sadness to Breville's plate, he had tried to listen carefully and caringly to me, and when he still felt he had not done enough for me, to help me through whatever pain I was going through, he had offered up the one thing he had to offer, which was the telephone number of his mother an entire state away. He had given me what he could think to give me on short notice, and sometime in the days after my visit and before today's phone call, he had called his mother and told her something—that I was going through a hard time, that I could use a friend, that he cared for me—and he had asked her to talk to me. And she had. Perhaps all the reserve I'd heard in her voice had been a response to the reserve she'd heard in my voice. I didn't know.

What I did know for certain was that I felt some of the same self-consciousness I'd felt in the visiting room the day Breville had sung to me. He'd offered up that goofy version of "Goodnight, Irene," and the thing was so corny I almost couldn't stand to listen to it. But there he'd sat in the visiting room among his fellow convicts, singing to me.

It was almost more than I could bear.

24

THE NEXT NIGHT I was lying in bed with Breville's latest letter
fanned out on the pillows in front of me. I'd gone for a swim for a
long time, and I felt cool in my skin and the light cotton nightgown
I wore. Breville's letter was from days ago, and I'd seen him since
I'd received it, but I still liked to have his pages in front of me. I
wanted to make sure I wrote about whatever he asked me about,
and it helped me connect with him as I wrote if I saw his words in
front of me.

This night I was trying to describe what my orgasms were like,
but I doubted if what I wanted to say would sound compelling to
anyone but me. I figured Breville would want to hear that a good
fuck made me come, but it wasn't the truth of my life, and it wasn't
what I wanted to write.

"The most intense orgasms I have are often the ones I have
alone," I wrote instead. "Not that I don't come with men—I do,
especially when they go down on me, and especially when they slip
a finger inside as they eat me. But for sheer intensity, the orgasms
I have when I masturbate with my vibrator win out. I have one
orgasm, and if I wait a couple minutes—just long enough for the

strongest contractions to subside, but before I come down from the mountain, so to speak—then I can have another orgasm and another. It is easy to come again and again, and there is no worrying about a partner, or worrying about being selfish. Which is not to say that I prefer being alone—I prefer being with a man and kissing and sharing all the closeness and passion. But I know my body, and I know how to come like that, over and over."

I was thinking what I could possibly write next when I heard someone pull into the driveway. It wasn't a driveway, really—just a patch of grass worn thin beside the cabin—but I heard the sound of the motor and saw the headlights shining. At first I thought it was someone who'd gotten lost and needed a place to turn around, but the engine shut off and the lights went out, and in the moonlight I could see the truck from the side window.

After the second knock, I opened the door of the cabin, but I kept the screen door latched.

"Can I come in?" the cowboy said.

I didn't answer but stood there in the doorway, watching him, watching the night air around him. I didn't turn on the light outside or in the kitchen. I didn't want him to see me, and I didn't want to see him. I just wanted to hear what he had to say.

"I would have been here earlier," he said. "But I forgot the way to your place. You're a hard person to find."

"You found me."

"Can I come in?"

I didn't say anything.

"You act like you don't know me," the cowboy said.

"I don't."

"But I know you."

"You don't know anything about me," I said. "I thought you were in Wyoming."

"I was. I came back to see you."

"Why not tell the truth?" I said. "Did your friends get tired of you? Throw you out?"

"I told you. I went back. Look at my eyes. I've been driving since yesterday. I need a fucking shower. I've driven up and down this road four or five times, trying to find this goddamn place."

"Maybe I don't want to be found."

"Jesus Christ, Suzanne."

"Well, at least you remember my name," I said. But I unhooked the screen door and let the cowboy step into the kitchen. And then I put on the light. I wanted to see exactly who was standing in front of me.

He was off crutches but still in a leg brace. Still limping. He stood, shaking his head. I just kept on looking at him.

"Here's what I think. I think you came down here tonight from Blackduck," I said. "I think your friends finally got sick of you and threw you out."

"You're pretty smart," he said. "But you have it all wrong."

"I'm smart enough," I said. "What part did I get wrong?"

"All of it."

"Okay, I don't know where you're living. All I know is the bars are closed now, and that's why you decided to come out here."

The cowboy half-stepped toward me then. And the next thing he did was slow, deliberate. I saw his arm moving, but it happened so gradually I didn't feel I had to move away, because I knew I could at any time. The cowboy reached toward me and slipped a couple fingers between my legs, pushing the cotton of my nightgown back against my vulva. And he kept his fingers there. Holding me.

"Is this bar closed?" he said. "Can I still get a drink?"

His hand felt hard, like a branch. Now that he was close, I could smell him. I didn't smell barroom so much as I smelled him: sweat, dirty shirt, that pelt of jet hair. He slipped his fingers back a little farther, making the cotton tight. His thumb was at the front of me.

"Is it closed?"

I didn't have to say yes or no. I just had to let his hand stay between my legs. I hadn't wanted him until he touched me, so I didn't know if it was just a hand I wanted, or him—cowboy, archangel.

Howling dog.

2 5

THE COWBOY STANK.

When we started screwing in the kitchen, I pushed myself up on my forearms on the windowsill and stood on my toes to let him inside me. He fucked me standing in his jeans and boots, but after a couple of minutes, he pulled away from me and we went to the bed.

That was when I really got a whiff of him—when he stripped down. I smelled old sweat, armpit stink, and someplace underneath, wood smoke. He smelled a little like my college boyfriend Phillip, who didn't change his shirts every day and whose scent could almost make me come, but he also smelled like Cree, my high school boyfriend, after he'd been camping.

But the cowboy was not Phillip and he was not Cree. He was entirely himself.

"You smell like meat," I said when I got near him. He went to pull me on top of him, but I pushed him away. I buried my nose in his side and licked up his skin to the damp hair under his arm. He was bitter.

His cock was bitter, too. Not the drop of semen at the end—but his head and shaft. First I tasted myself, like salt, since we'd fucked in the kitchen, and then I tasted him.

"Goddamn it," he said after a little while. "Let me fuck you."

So I got his cock out of my mouth and then I climbed on top of him.

"Now I know you, too," I said.

2 6

THE NEXT DAY, after the cowboy left—back to Wyoming, or Black-duck, or wherever it was that he was living—I picked my letter to Breville up off the floor. I had no idea if I would see the cowboy again, but something in my body told me I would. I knew I hadn't had my fill of him, and I thought he felt the same way about me. Still, none of it was anything I could count on, and I didn't want to give up whatever friendship or flirtation I had with Breville in the meantime. If I added the two men together, one with his constancy and the other with his black kisses, I had something complete.

When I read what I'd written about my orgasms, it seemed obviously crazy to send it. Breville told me the guards read prisoners' letters, yet here I was writing about my sexuality to a convicted rapist in Stillwater state prison. But I remembered how Breville had held me the day I dropped in on him, how his voice had sounded when he called me sweet, and how he had offered me what he could when I felt bad. And I decided to finish the letter.

I wrote, "Sometimes it seems like my orgasm is a tiny animal inside me. It comes out when things are safe, when I feel relaxed. It's blue-green, and moist. Other times my orgasm isn't like that at all. It's a rushed, pressing thing. I try to get my body to come before the man does, try to hold myself up on one arm and come on his cock." Last night I'd come that way with the cowboy: kneeling at the edge of the bed, holding myself up on one shoulder, working my vibrator so urgently my hand cramped, while he screwed me from behind, standing. My cunt was just the right height that way, and he could wear his leg brace. But of course I didn't put that in my letter to Breville.

"But that only stands to reason," I wrote instead. "Even if each of my orgasms is similar to others in some ways, each one is also different. And the ways to get to them are always different." But I didn't tell Breville more. I didn't tell him that I sometimes came in a matter of seconds if I'd been thinking of it long enough beforehand, or that my favorite fantasies when I masturbated were of women. I didn't say that some days this summer I masturbated two or three times, in part because the time itself was so intimate, filled with swimming, stripping down and toweling off, damp skin and hair. I didn't tell him that one day I had to hide in the corner of the cabin because I'd started to masturbate in the living room and had no clothing on when Merle had come knocking on the door. And I especially didn't tell Breville that it was my current thrill to think of my breasts being bound or having my nipples pinched hard enough to hurt. The thought of those two things alone was nearly enough to make me come.

It wasn't that I thought Breville wouldn't like hearing all of it—if he was anything like other men I'd known, my fantasies of redheaded women and bondage would excite him. I just didn't want to tell him. Those things were my private thoughts, and I didn't want to reveal them. While nothing I ever wrote to Breville was dishonest, it was calculated.

Besides, there were always things I held back from a man. Even with my rape, even as I was trying to sort through my rage with Breville so that I might one day leave it behind, there were things I didn't tell him about that night. But he was not the only person I withheld that information from—there were certain things I never told anyone. Not lovers, not friends, not the different therapists I'd seen over the years. For instance, I never told anyone about the worst part of my rape.

It wasn't the gonorrhea or herpes, and it wasn't the hard strokes of the fuck Frank L—— gave me. It was something he said to me when his penis was inside me.

Because I was dry, it burned each time he moved into me. It was like fire, it was like a knife—I didn't know how to describe the slicing, burning sensation. But I lay still, thinking it would hurt less if I didn't move.

"Good pussy doesn't just lie there," Frank L—— told me then.

And because I wanted it to be over, but mostly because I didn't want to be a bad lay and a lousy fuck, I began to move with him. I participated in my rape.

And that was the thing: because I had believed I was going out on a date, because I willingly got in the truck, because I was convinced on that day when I was sixteen that my main worth in the world was sexual, I believed I had to please my rapist. Him of the stinking hair and infected cock. And in that way, Frank L—— became king of my vagina, boss of my pussy, chief of my cunt.

That was the secret I shared only with my rapist. That was the thing I never told my friends or Breville.

2 7

I TRIED TO FULFILL at least some of Breville's request the next time I went to Stillwater. I wore a black dress that buttoned up the front. It came a little past my knees, but I left the bottom two buttons unbuttoned. While I was standing still or walking slowly, the dress really looked no different than it would have if I'd buttoned it all the way. It didn't look different until I was sitting down in the visiting room chairs, beneath the spider plant, across from Breville.

After we sat down, after I looked at the buttons on my dress and then at Breville, he said, "Open a couple more."

"How was your week? How have you been?" I said, crossing my legs. When my one knee was up on the other, I passed my fingers over a button and slid it out of its hole.

After Breville replied, I went on. "I swam across the lake yesterday," I said, opening another button as I talked. "One of the people who lives over there gave me a ride home. She couldn't believe I swam all that way."

Keeping my eyes on Breville's face, I uncrossed my legs and slowly moved my knees apart so he could see more of my thighs and black panties.

I thought Breville would say something then—would compliment me or respond in some way. But he was silent. I could see from his face it all meant something, and that whatever was going on inside him was powerful. But his silence still embarrassed me.

"Do you like it?" I said, but my throat was tight and my voice didn't sound right.

"More than you know."

"Tell me a story," I said then, pushing my shoulders down, trying to relax. "Tell me about the time you were in California, when you saw the Pacific. Didn't you go to San Diego? Am I remembering that right?"

"What do you want to know?"

"Anything. Anything you want to tell me. How did you get out there?"

"I hitchhiked. I hitchhiked until I got to San Diego. And then I hitchhiked home."

"You didn't want to stay?"

"No, no. I don't know. Maybe," Breville said, his voice evening out a little. "I had nothing except the clothes on my back. Someone stole the rest of my stuff. Even my shoes."

"What do you mean?"

"The guy I was hitching with. When we pulled into a rest stop, I went to the bathroom, and when I came out, there he was, pulling away with all my shit. I had nothing but shorts and a T-shirt. A pair of flip-flops. He left me standing there."

"God, weren't you pissed?"

"Course I was. But what do you expect? There's no honor among thieves," Breville said. "I probably would have done the same thing to him, if I could have."

He stretched his arms then and spread his legs wide open so they could be on the outside of mine. Then he slouched down in his chair and kept looking between my legs.

"I think the guy wanted to make a pass at me," Breville said. "And when he saw that wouldn't work, he stole from me."

He brought one leg inside the angle of mine and bent down to tie his shoe. As he was tying, he stared down the tunnel of my thighs.

"I wish I could see it," he said.

I looked at his face after he said that, but I didn't know if he meant he wished he could touch me and be with me like a normal person, like a lover, or if he just meant he wished I hadn't worn panties. I could have asked, and maybe I was going to ask.

"Do you ever shave it?" Breville said.

It took me a moment, but then I said, "No. No. It's not my thing."

"Did you ever think about it?"

"Not really," I said. "People can either take me the way I am or they can leave me."

"I shouldn't have asked you that. I'm sorry."

"You can ask. I'm just telling you the truth."

"No, I shouldn't have asked. Not here. Not like this."

We sat silently for a moment, and when Breville looked away to the guard's table, I inched my legs back together.

"I heard from that lawyer the other day," he said when he turned back to me.

"What did he say?"

"He said I should try an appeal. That my case had merit. That I got bad legal advice to begin with."

"He told you that?"

"I knew it all along," Breville said. "If I'd pled guilty, I'd be out of here by now. It's not like I killed anyone."

When he said that, everything inside the room just stopped. Just stopped. I understood Breville was talking solely about his case, and I understood he had already served longer than the

mandatory minimum state sentence for rape. But the words bothered me. Stuck inside me.

"Oh, I don't know," I said. "I think something died in me after
my rape."

Breville looked at me, and almost without pause, he said, "I felt
that way too. After the rape."

And I did not know what to say after that, either, because I
didn't know if he was telling me a part of him had died after he
raped the woman in South Minneapolis, or if he had himself been
raped in prison. I didn't know, and for the second time that day, I
didn't ask Breville exactly what he meant.

It seemed neither one of us knew where to go after the com-
ment. The rest of what we talked about was idle chatter. Nothing of
consequence.

Just before Breville and I left our chairs to say goodbye in the
taped-off square, he said, "Can I see it one more time?"

He again bent to tie his shoe and fix his pant leg. Again he looked
down the channel of my thighs to my black panties. And when he sat
up, he looked from his lap to my eyes and back to his cock. This
time I knew the language well enough. And when Breville lifted his
chin to me, his lips parted slightly, I understood that, too.

He must have wanted me to be sure, though, because he said,
"Good enough to eat."

I didn't know how to feel when he said that. I felt confused by
everything that had just passed between us. But a shiver went
through me. I could not explain it because I did not feel comfortable or at ease, but there was this current that kept flowing out from
Breville to me. Over to me and over me.

When Breville and I held each other in front of the guard that
day, he said into my hair, "I'm falling in love with you."

"Are you?" I said. And then we were pulling away from each
other.

thief

When we turned the last time to see each other before we each walked through our respective doors, Breville put his hand out to make the pass through the air as he usually did. When I put my hand out, though, I didn't hold it flat to make the *Steady* motion. Instead I held my hand in the air, palm toward him. As if I were touching his chest, touching his skin. And Breville nodded. Three or four small, nearly imperceptible nods, but I saw them. And I knew he understood that I felt something for him, too. Even if I could not say, I felt it.

28

THE MORNING AFTER I came back from the Cities, Merle stopped at the cabin on one of his walks. He was wearing a jacket and his Kubota cap, even though it was already about eighty degrees out.

"Sorry to bother," he said. "I was just wondering if you were around last night."

"I was down in the Cities and got in late," I said. "Why?"

"Well, I was away for most of the evening, and when I came home, my garage door was open."

"And you didn't leave it open?"

"Never do," he said. "I just wondered if you saw anything. Heard anything."

"I can't say I did."

"Strange. I just never leave that door open and there it was, standing open."

"Does it worry you?"

"Oh, I'm not sure there's anything to worry about," he said. "I just found it notable."

"Well," I said, "I'll try to be on the lookout."

"I also wanted to tell you they're looking for a teacher, over to the high school."

"What kind of teacher?"

"Your kind," Merle said. "English, I mean. You can read it yourself. It's in the paper."

When I said I hadn't bought the paper that week, he made me walk with him back to his place so he could get his copy out of the kindling box.

"I guess I might not find out who was in my garage," Merle said as we walked.

"I don't know what to tell you," I said. "And they didn't take anything?"

"No, not that I can see. I just thought I'd ask. In case you heard something."

There was a part of me that wondered if the cowboy had been back. But even if he had been, and even if he'd been looking for me, what possible reason would he have for going up the road to Merle's or for opening the garage door? It made no sense, and I chalked up the little nagging feeling in the back of my mind to my wariness and to Merle's questions.

In fact, the whole conversation made me wonder what Merle was trying to get at. He walked the road at all times, several times a day, and he would have seen the cowboy's truck at the cabin. Would have heard him, too. Each time the cowboy was here, we screwed long into the afternoon, and each time he came, he'd done his coyote howling. Even though the cabin was set back a ways from the road, who knew what Merle had heard?

"Thanks for the paper," I said then, my hand on the screen door. "I'll bring it back when I'm done."

He waved his hand. "No need," he said. "Keep it. I have plenty."

When he said that, he sounded like himself, but his eyes were impossible to read under the cap. I told myself there wasn't anything more to the conversation except someone fretting about a door left open when it shouldn't have been. And if there was more, I couldn't do anything about it anyway.

That night when I came from a swim, the phone was ringing. When I answered, it took a second for the recorded voice to begin saying, "This is a collect call from an inmate at a Minnesota correctional facility."

When the voice was done, I said, "Hey, how are you?"

"I'm sorry I'm calling," Breville said. "You know I don't like to call and stick you with the bill."

"It's okay. What's going on?"

"You should know it's usually bad news with me," he said. "Do you have time for this?"

"I have time."

"All right, then. I'll just come out with it. I talked to my counselor today. About you. About us. I don't want to tell you what she said. But I have to. I have to. She always tells me the truth, you know?"

"What did she say?"

"She said this was a false relationship. What you and I have. It's an artificial relationship."

I didn't say anything for a moment, and then I said, "Artificial?"

"Because there's no way for us to share experiences together. There's no way for us to do things together," Breville said. "It's not a real relationship. That's what she told me."

"Well," I said. "I think she's probably right."

"Jesus, I was afraid you'd say that."

"Well, you can't share anything with anyone," I said. "Not while you're in prison. But does that mean you're supposed to go without friendship?"

"It's not friendship I talked to her about. I told her I had feelings for you."

"What else did you tell her?"

"That I cared for you, and that you were making a difference in my life."

"Did you tell her about my rape?"

"I didn't say anything about that."

"You might want to," I said. "You might as well be honest."

"I don't know. It would probably just make it worse. What she says—do you really think it's artificial? What's between us?"

"I think probably it is," I said. "But it still means something to me."

"Does it?"

"Doesn't it mean something to you?"

"You know it does," Breville said. "But this person, she's never steered me wrong."

"I think you should listen to her."

"I do listen to her, but it's depressing. I could have been out this year. If I'd pled guilty. I did this to myself. Do you know that?"

"I know," I said. "You told me. And I'm sure you agonize over it. I bet you never stop."

"Yeah, so you know that, too."

"It would be impossible for me not to know that."

Breville made a noise into the phone then that I didn't have a word for. A short moan, a sigh, a bark—I wasn't sure.

I waited for him to say something more, but instead I heard an alarm go off in the background.

"I have to go," Breville said. "Bed check. Write me."

Before I could respond, though, the line went dead.

It didn't matter. We'd both said everything there was to say. I'd heard enough of Breville's voice to know that whatever he was feeling, whatever he was going through, was so private and deep nothing could touch it. There was no respite from it. It reminded me of the Stephen Crane poem that went:

I eat it because it is bitter
And because it is my heart.

And maybe there was no connection between Breville's regret and my own—he was a rapist and I'd been raped. Two opposites. But I still felt like I knew something about the remorse he felt. There was a piece of tape I played in my own head, over and over, from the night I was raped. If only I'd chosen not to go out with Keil Ward that night. If only I'd balked in the parking lot and made some excuse to go back inside the restaurant. If only I'd stopped. But instead of telling Keil Ward I changed my mind, instead of saying, *No, I don't want to drop off your friend*, I got into the truck.

That was the moment I always thought of and always pictured in my mind. The moment when I stopped walking, when I was standing beside the truck in my white waitress uniform, when my hand was in Keil Ward's hand, when I did not know how to say, *I don't like your friend*, when I did not know how not to do the next thing. Then Keil was lifting me and Frank L—— was reaching for me and I was getting into the truck.

When I let myself, I could still see in my mind the parking lot lit by a streetlight, the rust-colored truck, the trash bins beside the side kitchen door of the restaurant. But even more than that, I could still remember exactly what it felt like to be my sixteen-year-old self. That night I was wearing my white polyester waitress uniform with a red apron I made on my mom's sewing machine, the front pockets big enough to hold a green guest-check pad and tips; white sneakers with rainbow stripes on the sides and small white socks with pink pom-poms; pantyhose, and panties inside my pantyhose; a white cable sweater that reminded me of my grandmother; no makeup; my hair long and taken down out of the ponytail I kept it pulled back in when I was working.

And when I let myself, I could imagine what my face must have looked like in those last few seconds before I stepped into Frank L——'s truck. My face would have revealed the apprehension I felt, and the doubt. My instinctual fear. I would have looked back over at the side kitchen door or the restaurant, but instead of making any excuse at all to Keil Ward and running toward that door, I got into Frank L——'s truck and did the thing I'd been trained to do. I cooperated and I performed.

By the time I got home that night, my panties were so rusty with blood that I wadded them up and hid them in the downstairs trash. I could imagine what my face must have looked like when I peered down at the blood, but what's more, I could still feel the look in my face all these years later.

My panties weren't the only piece of clothing I lost that night. In my distress after the rape, I'd left my pantyhose and pom-pom socks in the truck, along with the sweater that reminded me of my grandmother. I could still feel a flicker pass over my face when I remembered leaving those things behind in Frank L——'s truck, or when I recalled the moment I realized it didn't matter, that none of the things that used to mean something to me mattered at all.

I could remember—imagine in my mind—everything about that night. I still saw the color of the truck, the savage way Frank L—— ate my pussy, the bleached and medicinal smell of Keil Ward's cock. The only thing I didn't have a clear picture of was Frank L——'s face.

I never asked myself to imagine that.

Once, though, when I was in downtown Minneapolis, I saw a man with greasy blond hair, a snub-nosed face, a mustache worn to camouflage rotting teeth. He was in a cheap blue windbreaker, and though I knew I didn't know him—had never seen him before in my life—my stomach clenched into a knot.

That's when I remembered what Frank L—— looked like.

29

BREVILLE SOUNDED SO DISTRAUGHT when he told me what his counselor said, I was sure he would call me back the next night, but he didn't. And when no letter came the next day, or the next, I decided to drive down to Stillwater to see him.

But instead of hearing the guard announce over the intercom, "Visit for Breville," I heard my own name called. When I came up the counter, the guard, a woman, told me Breville was on lockdown that day and could not get any visits.

"Did something happen?" I said.

"I can't tell you. All I'm able to tell you is that he is on lockdown and cannot receive visitors."

Breville told me they sometimes locked down different wings of the prison and searched prisoners' cells if they suspected people of possessing contraband, and sometimes the entire population was placed on lockdown if there was some kind of upheaval or if things got violent. But since other visitors were being processed through the waiting room, I knew it wasn't that kind of general lockdown. I wanted to ask the guard more but I knew she couldn't tell me anything, and I knew I was holding things up. So I turned away and got my purse out of the locker and exited through the huge doors of the prison waiting room. And was left with the day on my hands.

I could have called Julian and made him come out to lunch with me or gotten right back on the freeway to head north. But I did neither. Instead, I did something I could have done and perhaps should have done weeks ago: I drove to the Hennepin County Courthouse, where I could read the case file of Breville's trial.

I didn't know why I chose that particular day to go to the courthouse. Maybe it was the reality of hearing about what Breville's counselor had told him about the artificiality of our relationship, or maybe knowing Breville was on lockdown frightened me—I wasn't sure. I'd always known I could read the file, but I hadn't wanted to. But now I needed to see for myself what had happened at his trial, and I wanted to read about it in the court records and not in Breville's handwriting. I wanted that distance and clarity. My visits to Stillwater had made his punishment perfectly visceral and clear, but the only information I had about his actual crime came from his admission, his words. It wasn't enough anymore.

And the first thing I understood from reading the transcripts of the grand jury and the trial was that Breville had been entirely honest with me about the rape. Though it was disorienting to read the information from an objective, third-person perspective, everything in those documents was absolutely familiar to me. The transcripts told the exact same story of the night that Breville had related to me in his letters and conversations, and it meant something to me to see how scrupulous he'd been in telling me the truth. But that did not make the documents any easier to read. His crime and a portion of his life were public record, and that alone separated Breville from the rest of society. No spider plant gently touching down on my hair or visible gallantry within the confines of the visiting room at Stillwater could alter that demarcation, the three separate felony counts on which he had been convicted, or the particular details of the rape. He had broken into a woman's house as she was sleeping. As she was sleeping.

I had been prepared to read all those things, at least in some way. What I had not been prepared for—what did not become clear to me until I stood at the counter of the Hennepin County Courthouse—was the arrogance and delusion it took for Breville to plead innocent.

He had told me he'd still been in denial at the time of the trial, and that he'd believed there was a way for him to "beat" the charge because his DNA had never been found. He believed that even though he'd had some of the woman's property in his possession at the time of his arrest. He told me all these things himself. But to read the court papers and see for myself how he'd gone through the entire trial denying the rape, denying the woman's story—her testimony—was something altogether different. Breville's declaration of his innocence made him seem more dangerous than if he had confessed outright that he was a rapist.

The trial was disastrous for him. I did not know what adjective to use for what it must have been like for the woman from South Minneapolis, but for Breville it was ruinous. His lies and refusal to admit guilt made him seem remorseless, devoid of conscience. That, on top of the invasiveness and violence of the crime itself, must have been what prompted the judge to increase the length of Breville's sentence from seven to fourteen years. After reading the transcript of the trial, the extended sentence made perfect sense to me in a way it hadn't before, even when Breville spelled it out for me. It wasn't that Breville had lied to me or misled me—I was the one who'd chosen to believe in his charm and his intelligence. His grace.

As I paged one last time through the file, my face felt tight, and something throbbed behind my right eye. I was tired from my drive, but of course it was more than that. I felt a kind of devastation, and I felt it through my whole body. If it weren't for Breville, the woman in South Minneapolis wouldn't have had her life altered as she did. She would have gone on dreaming that night in her own bed, would have gone on living just as she had before. Each moment of pain and fear she felt during the rape and every wave of disruption she experienced afterward was entirely Breville's fault.

I both identified with the woman in South Minneapolis and saw myself as being different from her. What had happened to me at sixteen was brutal and life-altering, but it was somehow less than what she had experienced. Breville broke into her house, fractured her sleep, and assaulted her in her own home, which was something much worse than I had gone through. I could sleep, at least when I was alone, but I wondered if she was always listening for the noise that had been him.

After closing the file and returning it to the clerk, I felt as though I couldn't see. I waited awhile by the courthouse door, until I lost the sensation of dizziness, but when I got to my car I turned the air conditioner on as high as it would go, and I sat there. It took me a minute to understand that underneath my panic I was feeling overwhelming grief. Grief about the rape of the woman in South Minneapolis as well as the old crushing sorrow I always felt about my own actions. Even though Breville had made me see the randomness of my own rape, knowing that I'd opened myself to its occurrence still produced desolation in me. That the woman in South Minneapolis had done nothing at all except wake from a dream—that was devastating to me. And I did not know where to go with my understanding and my grief. And my grief.

A few things became clear to me on the way home, over the 250 miles and four hours. It was clear to me Breville would have gone on injuring others if he had not been sent to prison, and it was clear prison had been his bitter salvation. Yet he was still appealing his sentence, and he was still able to say of his crime, *It's not like I killed anyone.* It made me wonder if he'd really changed at all from the time of his trial, or if the same insolence that had made him plead innocent still remained.

And if Breville—clean, sober, repentant—was in fact now a different man than the one I had read about in the court transcript, where had his older self gone? Had it been subsumed in his new personality? Was it there alongside and only hidden because of prison? I knew people changed all the time: they got older, lost interests and found them, grew antipathies, discovered passions. But it was almost impossible for me to believe Breville was wholly different from who he'd been at nineteen—something of his essential self had to remain the same. If enough of his ways of thinking and acting had changed, did it matter if some core of him was the same? I thought it did matter. If anyone knew how difficult it was to change in a deep and real way, it was me.

Though I kept pushing it from my mind, one other thing became wholly clear to me as I drove home. I kept thinking back to the day I met Breville, when he told me the love of his mother and father and grandfather weren't enough to help him, and to the day he told me he lost his virginity to his molesting twelve-year-old cousin. I now understood just how fully he'd told me the truth. Nothing could have counteracted the sexual abuse, the years of underage drinking, the petty thievery, or the violence and chaos he'd lived within. Breville had begun a certain course so early on that his life could only follow one path.

On the long drive home it became entirely clear to me that the surprising thing was not that Breville had raped someone when he was nineteen. The only surprise would have been if he had not become a rapist.

30

WHEN I GOT BACK TO THE CABIN, I saw Merle standing at the end of his driveway, talking to someone leaning up against a pickup pulled off to the side of the road. After he saw it was me, he waved me over.

I pulled into the end of the drive and Merle said, "Did you hear the news?"

"I'm just now getting home," I said. "What news?"

"Someone set a fire down at the old Churchill place. That's just down the road."

"They set a fire? To a building?"

"A house," the man leaning up against the pickup said. "Someone set it and they think they might have caught the guy. They found someone walking down the road nearby."

"He wasn't in his right mind," Merle said.

"Who was it?"

"No one around here knows him," Merle said. "A guy out of Thief River Falls."

I felt something in me fall a little bit, and I said to Merle, "Do you think that's who was in your garage the other day?"

"Might have been."

"What was he doing down here?" I said.

"No one knows," the man leaning up against the pickup told me. "No one knows him. He was just out wandering. No vehicle. Just walking."

But to me, it was a relief to hear that particular detail. Whatever desperate state the cowboy was in, I doubted he would have given up his truck, just as I doubted his troubled nature would come out in the form of arson. There were more disturbed people in the north woods than just him. But the story made me feel funny in a new way: it made me wonder about the night swims I took, and about being as isolated as I was in the cabin.

"What time did it happen? When did he set the fire?"

"This morning," Merle said. "But they're not sure it was this fellow. Could have been someone else."

"I think it must have been him," the pickup leaner said. "That guy set the fire and then he walked down the road in broad daylight."

We all shook our heads then and looked out at the blue lake and the falling dark.

I was only inside the cabin a few minutes when the phone began to ring. I heard the recorded voice say, "This is a phone call from an inmate at a Minnesota correctional facility," but when the spot came for Breville to say his name so I could accept or decline the call, a man's voice said, "Gates for Breville."

"Hello?"

"Hello, I'm calling for Alpha Breville. This is his friend Gates, and he asked me to call you."

"All right."

"I promise to keep it quick. He was sick today so they had him on lockdown."

"So he knows I came to visit him?"

"Yes, he does. He gave me your number and asked me to tell you what happened. He'll explain it all tomorrow."

"He'll be out of lockdown then?"

"Yes, he will. He'll tell you all about it."

"He's okay, then?"

"Yes, he's fine. He said he'll tell you all about it."

"All right, then," I said. "I understand. Thank you."

"No problem."

The line went dead before I could ask or say anything more. Not that I would have asked more—the rushed way Gates spoke prevented it. But the call unsettled me, and I was still thinking about it as I walked down to the lake to swim.

Sometimes during a late swim I felt exhilarated, but tonight I just wanted to swim out into the blackness and stop thinking. Once I was in the water, I tried to relax and let the lake cradle me, but the day kept intruding on my thoughts—being turned away at the prison, the trip to the courthouse, reading the transcript of Breville's trial, finding out about the fire, the odd tone of Gates's voice on the phone. I wished I had been able to talk to Breville, but if I had, I didn't know what I would have talked about. I didn't know if I wanted to tell him I'd gone to the courthouse to read his court file. Even though the documents were public record, I felt as if I had looked at something personal and private. I understood why I did it and thought I was right to do it, but I still didn't know if I wanted to admit it to Breville.

I didn't know what he would be able to say anyway. He'd told me truthfully about his crime, he told me he'd changed and that he was no longer the person he was when he raped, or even when he was tried for the crime. Since I could never see Breville in any situation other than the visiting room, and since I had no way of knowing anything about him except what he chose to divulge in letters or what I observed during a visit, I could only take him at his word about who he'd become since the trial. Words could be meaningless if they weren't backed by action, if they had no context. But the relationship I had with Breville was made up only of words, talk, and letters, and that was what made it artificial and false—exactly what his counselor had said.

Yet something real had happened between us. It had happened when I wrote about my rape and when he wrote back, and it happened every time I sat across from Breville in the visiting room, when his dark eyes met mine. It was not just the understanding I gained from Breville about my own rape, though he had given me insight, and it was not just sexual tension, though that flowed like a current between us, and it was not just the strangeness of the prison in Stillwater, though I knew myself well enough to admit I found the place powerful in its foreignness and danger.

It was something more complicated in its details, and no matter how long I looked at it, I could not get a clear picture.

Because of Breville, I'd been forced to think about what happened between people as they came together, the lines negotiated and crossed, the boundaries declared and transgressed, the mix of offering and taking. For instance, I liked men who took certain things without asking, like kisses and particular intimacies—and who would never dream of making other presumptions, such as wanting me to go to their church or have their children. I didn't generally like rough sex, but once in a while I did, and I always liked men who kissed hard and expertly. There was a cocksureness I desired in a man, a crudeness that pleased me, but there were a thousand ways for that to go wrong, just as there had been when I was sixteen.

And while it seemed impossible at thirty-three to describe any decision I made as a teenager as a choice, I knew that I was, at sixteen, capable of intense feeling and thought, and the night I was raped, I did make a choice. I wanted something from Keil Ward: attention, hard but tender kisses, excitement—a fuck. If he had just been who he seemed to be, if he had just given me the things I was looking for, the night would have turned out differently, as my story now would be different.

That was why, even though I had allowed Breville to convince me of the randomness of the rape, I could never fully lose the feeling that I was somehow complicit. Not in the lie that led up to the rape or in the savagery that was worked out on my body, but complicit because I had been seeking something that night. I was not like the woman Breville had raped in South Minneapolis, innocently asleep in my bed, assaulted by a stranger. And yet—and yet—the thing I had been seeking, the thing I had consented to, was entirely different than what had taken place. I had been willing to fuck and be fucked by Keil Ward that night, but I had not been willing to be raped. When I thought of that, the picture would go upside down again.

But that was what I meant by complicity.

Whatever my life had been in the past, it now was entirely my own choosing—a result of my tastes and predilections, my abilities and incapacities. I didn't know what I wanted from Breville anymore. I didn't know if the cowboy was some odd kind of soul mate or just another misfit. I didn't know if any of it even mattered. None of it was anything I could live my life by.

Since I couldn't push the events of the day from my mind—not Breville, not Merle's news of the fire or the phrase he had used to describe the man who set it, that he wasn't in his "right mind"—I gave up on floating. Instead, I swam as hard as I could, American crawl, a hundred strokes out and a hundred strokes back, again and again. And after a while I couldn't think about anything except the dark water and the moon, my own breathing, and the beating of my heart.

3 1

"I FUCKED UP, SUZANNE. I'm sorry."

Those were the first words Breville said when the prerecorded message from the prison phone system finished playing.

"If I'd have known you were coming down here, I would have got up and gone to work no matter how sick I was. I swear to God."

"I know that," I said. "What was wrong?"

"I had a headache in the morning, so I didn't go to my job. They put you on lockdown when you don't report for work. I should have just gone."

"It's all right."

"I just made myself sick with things. I feel like I'm losing my way."

"Are you still upset over what your counselor told you? About us?"

"That. That and the appeal," he said. "But I always lose my balance. That's what Gates tells me."

"Why do you feel like you're losing your balance?"

"I'm not focused on my life in here. I get caught up in things out there and things here start to go wrong."

"How can you not think about things out here?" I said. "You're in prison and you want to get out."

"It doesn't matter what I want," he said, and I could hear the frustration in his voice. "My life is in here. I have to keep from getting caught up."

"What are you caught up in?" I said. "Are you caught up in me?"

"You. Trying to get this appeal going. It makes it harder. I don't know if you can understand. If this appeal doesn't go through, I'll be thirty-four by the time I get out."

"It's a long time," I said. "But thirty-four isn't old."

"You'll be forty," he said. "Do you think of that?"

"Not really," I said. "I've thought of it, but I don't go around thinking of it."

"Yeah, that's a good way to put it. That's good. I wish I could do that."

We were both quiet for a moment—not too long, or the system would cut us off—and then I said, "Would it be better if we weren't in contact?"

"That's exactly what I don't want."

"But if it makes your life harder—"

"Better. Better and harder," Breville said. "But it's my problem. I didn't mean to trouble you with it. Let's change the subject. Tell me what's going on with you."

"Okay," I said. "Okay. Today I had an interview for that job I applied for."

"Did you get it?"

"I don't know."

"They'll give it to you," Breville said. "You know they will. Who are they going to find who's better than you?"

"I don't know. But I don't have the job yet. And if they do offer it to me, I still have to decide if I want it."

"But you told me you wanted a change from your old job."

"I did. I do," I said. It wasn't a lie, but it wasn't exactly the truth.

I never told Breville about Richaux, or why I'd come up north. I never told him specifics about any of my old relationships, but I never told any man I was involved with about his predecessors.

"Well, then, you'll have a change," Breville went. "You'll be up there for good."

"I can come down to visit."

"How can you do that when you're working?"

"The weekends," I said.

"You know what makes me sick? It just makes me sick to think that you came all the way down here yesterday and I missed you."

"It's okay," I said.

"It was a waste for you."

"It's fine," I said. "Things happen. I'm just glad nothing's wrong. And I don't want to make your life harder. I'm sorry if I'm doing that."

"No, no," Breville said. "You make me want to try for things. Things I can't get. But it's up to me to find the balance. I have to learn not to lose focus on what I'm doing in here. This is my life. I can't let myself get carried away."

"I don't know," I said. "Maybe it's all just too much."

"It's not too much. It's what I want. It's what I want in ways I can't hardly say."

"Could you write it to me?"

"I'll try. I'll try to do that."

"I'll try, too," I said.

"You don't have to try. Don't you get it? You're perfect. I'm the one who has to try."

"Everyone has to try," I said.

The fifteen-second warning tone sounded then.

"Write to me," I said.

"You write to me, too, Suzanne," he said. And then the line cut off.

After I hung up, I thought about what Breville had said about losing his balance, about how he was getting too caught up in things other than his life in Stillwater. When he said it, I thought he must be joking, because what kind of life did he have in prison? But of course he did have a life there. Whatever his days were like, they contained interactions, relationships, negotiations, tensions, activities, periods of boredom, as well as expectations met and unmet—just as my days did, just as anyone's did. What I heard him say was that his focus on things outside of Stillwater produced a kind of conflict for him, and made it harder for him to be in the place he occupied and would occupy for the next seven years. In certain ways his relationship with me was positive, but in other ways I made his life more complicated and took away from his ability to live his life in prison.

There was a part of me that found it incredible. Ludicrous, even. Breville did not have to worry about paying for rent or car insurance, he did not have to keep clothes on his back or food in the fridge, he did not have to pay bills except the one he could pay for his local telephone calls. Certainly his life was filled with stress and violence, but on another level it was completely removed from the pressures other people dealt with on a daily basis. Yet who would willingly trade their pressures for the ones Breville faced? As crazy as what Breville had said first sounded, I had to accept that just as I had a rich and full existence outside of my calculated, constricted relationship with him in the visiting room, he, too, had a complex life right there in Stillwater state prison.

I don't know why it surprised me so much to realize that—he'd given me enough glimpses. There were the dinners he cooked for himself and other men on the wing, his friendship with Gates, the associate's degree he earned in prison college classes, the things he did in his spare time. One day when we were working to find things to talk about in the visiting room, he told me that in the last week, he'd read *Get Shorty* and watched *Little Women* on TV.

"*Little Women?*" I asked.

"Sure. It was a good story."

The conversation surprised me, and I liked that. I liked both the surprise and the potential it made me see in Breville.

He'd done the same thing tonight—surprised me. I knew I was older than he was by seven years—we'd talked about it a couple of times, but I hadn't realized how much it was on his mind. Maybe I discounted it because I blithely believed what he told me when the issue came up, that age didn't matter to him, and that I didn't look my age anyway. Or maybe I figured he didn't have the widest range of women to choose from, sitting there in Stillwater state prison, and that he should be happy I was involved with him. Tonight, though, I realized Breville did think about it. It was part of his calculations and it somehow mattered to him. Maybe he just had the myopia of someone in his twenties who believed everyone age forty and up was old—I didn't know. But whatever Breville thought about our respective ages, the conversation made me realize he thought about a future with me.

But I did not think about a future with him.

32

AS IT TURNED OUT, whatever Merle heard or did not hear from the cabin the nights I spent with the cowboy didn't stop him from offering to rent me his house when I got the job at the local school. He was going to Arizona that winter with all the other snowbirds.

"That way I won't have to worry about this place," Merle said. "You'd be here to keep an eye on things."

I was as surprised by Merle's offer as I had been by the job offer itself. I didn't have any of my school clothes up at the cabin, so I'd dressed for the interview in jeans and the nicest blouse I could find at the Pamida store in town, and the director of the program had talked to me for about forty-five minutes. I was offered the job the next day. To make an offer so quickly based on such a short interview made me figure the place was desperate, or that the guy wanted to make a decision and get on with his summer. But something in me wanted to give the job a try. The position was at an alternative program for at-risk students, and if the place really was a safety net for kids as the director claimed, I thought it might work. During the interview, the director kept saying, "Our bottom line is kids," and I figured if everyone was as sincere or as innocuous as he seemed to be, I'd be just fine. Or at least fine enough.

"Put it this way," Merle said. "You'd be doing me a favor by staying in the house."

"I haven't said yes to them yet."

"But you're going to, aren't you?"

"I don't know. I think so."

"Well, I usually leave for Phoenix around October fifteenth, but maybe this year I can go a little earlier. I could head out at the end of September. How does that sound?"

"If I do say yes, I can stay here," I said, nodding back at the cabin. "It won't get that cold."

"You'd be surprised."

"So I'll bring all my quilts," I said. "Don't change your plans on my account."

"No one's changing any plans," Merle said. "I do what I please. Besides, it's one way to get a woman into this house."

He looked away as he said it, but then he looked sideways at me from under the Kubota cap.

I thought of all the times he'd stopped to talk to me when I was in the yard or down on the dock. At other times, though—when he saw me with a book or notebook, or when it looked like I was dozing down by the water, or if I was sitting off under the trees at the side of the cabin having a cup of coffee in the morning—he kept on his walk, not stopping or even slowing. He never once intruded. After one storm, when a couple of trees had fallen across the road, he drove down to the cabin as soon as the worst lightning had passed to make sure I was all right. Of course, I thought. Of course. I thought of him as an old man because he was retired, but he was probably seventy at the most. Old enough to be a father figure— or not.

"You're good to me, Merle," I said then. From his face I saw it was the right thing to say.

When I told Julian the news that night, he said, "Why do you want to bury yourself alive in the north woods?"

"You know I need a change."

"I thought you were getting a change this summer."

"It was a trial run. Now I see it's the right thing."

"So, I guess I'm stuck with your sofa in my basement."

I said, "I promise I will come and get my shit."

"Actually, I sort of like having a sofa in the basement. I can sit down there while I'm doing laundry."

"Then I give you the gift of that sofa," I said. "You know there's a board broken in the back of the frame. I broke it when I fucked Richaux on it."

"You couldn't screw him in your bed?"

"He liked to be able to watch TV while we did it."

"Jesus," Julian said, laughing. "Too much information."

"Seriously, I want you to think I'm doing the right thing. And I want you to be happy for me."

"I am happy for you. I am happy about whatever makes you happy. You know that."

"I know that."

"Just wait, in a year you'll be married to a logger," he said, and I could hear him inhale on a cigarette. "Then you'll call me up crying when he hangs a dead deer in your backyard or tracks mud on your kitchen floor."

"Julian."

"You'll get tired of those north woods types. I know what I'm talking about."

And he did. He hadn't always been Julian, and he hadn't always lived in a bungalow in Edina. Forty-five years ago he'd been born on a farm in Bagley, Minnesota, and named Lyle. One of six kids. If anyone knew the art of transforming, he did.

"I'll see you soon," I said. "I'll clear everything out of your house but the sofa."

"Absolutely," Julian went. "Pencil me in after your convict."

"I will," I said. "I love."

"I love, too."

I wrote a letter of resignation to my old school that night, and the next morning I drove to town, to the post office, to send it by registered mail. And that's how I stepped free of my old life in the Cities, or the concrete box, as Merle called the place.

33

THE NEXT DAY a letter came, and I could see from the date it was out of sync. Breville had written it days ago, right after our last visit together, before the night he'd been so distraught, and before I'd driven down to Stillwater and been turned away by the guard. In the letter Breville said he wanted to apologize for what he'd asked me the last time I'd come to see him. At first I didn't remember what he'd asked, but I kept reading and I remembered.

He wrote:

I could see from your reaction you were mad when I asked about it. I don't blame you. I don't think I would like it much if I was a girl either. It must be a guy thing, wanting to see that hidden part of a woman's body. When one girl shaved it for me in the past, what I liked about it best was seeing her lips. I knew they were called that, but I didn't really get it until I saw them, until they were bare. I just wanted to run my fingers and mouth over them all day! But I will be honest with you, I do think about you that way and I wonder what your body looks like and what it would feel like. I hope you can understand, you are the woman in my life. I already know those "lips" would be as pretty as the ones you brush against my cheek every time you say hello and good-bye, but I couldn't stop myself from asking you if you'd ever done it. Sick, I know. You come all the way down here and that's how I talk to you in that room. But my sex life is a fantasy life right now and you are my fantasy, Suzanne. I want to know everything about you. What you look like when you sleep, what you look like there. Sometimes that's how I get through the day here, picturing it. Honest to Christ I hope I'm not making things worse by saying that, but it's the truth. Do you think you could ever be interested? Do you think it could ever be exciting to you? Because I would love to think of you that way.

I had started reading Breville's letter the way I usually did, walking the gravel road back to the cabin. But when I got to that part, I stopped. My body heated up and I felt light-headed. I felt like I could hear Breville saying the words to me, as if I could see his face as he said them. I stood on the edge of the road until I finished the letter.

Once I got inside the cabin, I took off my clothes and dug through the bathroom drawer for all my pink razors. I felt like I was shaking, and I was still light-headed. I couldn't explain it. Other men had talked about it before, but I always told them off—I didn't like the bare, little-girl idea of it. Yet here I was, nicking my fingers for Breville.

Breville.

I propped the mirror against the dresser, but it was still hard for me to see what I was doing. I started with the scissors, but I was up to the razor part now, pulling the skin taut with one hand and scraping with the other. My neck ached from bending over, so I stopped for a second and wished he could see how much trouble I was going to. As soon as I thought of him, though, I got the hot, quick feeling all over again, and I kept on.

When I finished the job, my skin felt tender—no doubt from all the scraping, but also because my protection was gone. I felt raw inside my panties, and my jeans seemed like armor when I pulled them back on. Even inside my clothes, I felt too present in the world. I walked around for a while, trying to get used to the feeling, but after a bit I gave up. I took off my clothes again and put on my softest nightgown. The cotton was a comfort. But I understood what Breville meant about how soft the skin was. It was softer than anything I'd ever touched.

It'll grow back, I told myself. And I let myself sleep.

The sun was low in the sky by the time I walked down to the dock to swim. For a second I wondered if the water would make the shaved place between my legs burn, but nothing hurt when I slid down into the water. After a few moments, I realized what I should have known all along: lake water never stung or burned, not even when I opened my eyes underwater and looked up to the sky. There wasn't anything in it to burn. The water was clean enough to drink, though I never had, except for the stray mouthful I swallowed when a boat wake hit me or I stuttered through a swimming stroke. If anything, the lake water soothed me. So I swam out until I was over the deepest part—eighty feet down to the bottom, if the maps were to be believed—and then I turned to float.

There were no boats, or at least none that I heard when I tilted my head back and let water fill my ears. I kept my back straight and held my arms out at my sides at first, but then I let my body go limp. My arms and legs drifted down slightly, and it seemed like I was half sitting and half lying in the water. When I floated like that I couldn't ever get over the feeling that the whole lake was holding me up—all five and a half billion gallons of it. Even though I'd gone through the trouble to look up the size of the lake and calculate the gallons, the number didn't get at the feeling I had when I floated, which was the sensation of being held up by a great, dark thing, something that went on for a long, long time. It was like floating in the night sky and the Milky Way galaxy.

When I came back from the dock that evening, I peeled off my wet suit and stood looking at myself in the bedroom dresser mirror. The mirror was big and low, and I could see my bare vulva, which looked both familiar and disturbing. Familiar because it reminded me of what that triangular patch looked like when I was in fifth grade, and disturbing because I wasn't a ten-year-old girl. It was an unusual sensation to be ten years old and thirty-three at the same time, and I had to walk away from the mirror and pull on my cotton nightgown again.

I thought Breville might call that night at nine—his usual time—but he didn't. The silence made me feel foolish, like I was all dressed up with no place to go. But I did not feel so foolish that I couldn't lie on the sofa and play with my newly bare and lake-damp self for a few moments. And in another few moments I knew I had to go into the bedroom, to where my vibrator was, plugged in and ready.

Before I lay down, though, I got two clips from the bathroom. They weren't real nipple clamps, just two flowered hair clips from Target. But I figured they'd work. And they did. Their light pinch made everything more urgent, and between those sensations and the feeling I got when I touched my own skin, I came hard—once, twice, a third time. I thought the shaving might change how things felt, but it didn't. Yes, there was more air surrounding my orgasms, and a new sharpness, like someone had music on too loud, but the contractions and feeling of falling were the same. If anything, the experience of the orgasms was stronger, but I didn't know if that was a result of my bare skin or the chilly tightness I felt in my nipples.

But the main change was the one in my head. I felt vulnerable and exposed just as I knew I would, and I didn't like seeing my ten-year-old self when I looked in the mirror. But I also felt other things. Blatant. Straightforward. Even to me the silkiness was bewitching. The whole thing seemed to be some kind of declaration. But what exactly was I declaring? That I was willing to be seen? That I was willing to do something that someone asked? I didn't know. But it was a declaration I made on my own body.

On my skin.

34

WHEN BREVILLE CALLED the next night, I still wasn't over the bare sensation of my vulva, but the thrill I'd felt when I first read his letter came back. I could barely wait for the "This is a call from an inmate at a Minnesota correctional facility" message to play through.

"So, did you get it?"

"Your letter?" I said. "I just got it yesterday."

"No, did you get the job?"

"Oh, I did. I did get it. And I accepted it."

"I knew you would."

"I know, I know. And I guess I'm going to rent my neighbor's house when he goes away for the winter."

"Why can't you stay where you're at?"

"It's just a cabin. But I'm going to rent Merle's house."

"That's a good deal for him."

"It's a good deal for me."

"So you have it all worked out already," Breville went. "See? I told you. I'm happy for you."

But he sounded anything but happy. His voice was tight and

quiet. So I said, "Well, I did get your letter. And do you want me to cheer you up?"

"Cheer me up?"

"Yeah, do you want me to tell you something good?"

"Sure. Tell me something good."

"Well, the letter came yesterday, and I already did it."

"Did what?"

I didn't want to come out and say it. I thought he should be able to figure it out, plus I knew the phone call was recorded. So I said, "You know. The thing you talked about in your letter. The thing you apologized about asking for? I did it."

Breville waited awhile and then he asked, "What did you go and do that for?"

"I don't know," I said. "I thought you'd be happy."

"Happy? Why would I be happy when you're out there and I'm in here?"

I felt defensive then. Embarrassed. "I guess I wanted to try it," I said. "I wanted to see how it felt."

Again there was silence on the line. I wondered if something had happened in between the time Breville had written me the letter and now, or if I had entirely misunderstood.

"Well, you have to at least let me see it," Breville told me. He sounded tired as he said it, though, and I began to wonder why I'd gone through the trouble.

"The next time you visit," he said. "You can give me a little show."

"A show?"

"When are you coming down?"

"I was thinking about tomorrow, but I don't know."

"Come on Monday. It won't be as crowded. I'll lean over and tie a shoelace. Like I did last time."

"I don't know if I can walk in there like that."

"Don't worry," Breville said. "Plenty of women do it."

"Well, maybe you should ask one of them for a show."

"I'm just saying plenty of women flash their husbands. Their boyfriends. That's all I meant."

I didn't know why I was surprised. Of course Breville wouldn't want to just hear about it. Of course he'd want to see it.

"Maybe," I said. Yet even as I was saying it, I was figuring out which dress was heavy enough so it wouldn't cling to my ass. Dark enough so it wouldn't show damp.

After I got off the phone with Breville, I felt unsettled, and I kept on feeling that way even after I went for a long swim. I knew it was from the phone conversation and the plan Breville had cooked up, but I also felt odd because I kept feeling like I was being watched. That's how that four-inch bare patch made me feel—and I felt it even with clothes on. Most of the summer I hadn't missed the distractions of the Cities, but just then I wished I could go somewhere for a cup of coffee, or wander in a store that was open late— anything to get out of the cabin. I knew there would be nothing open in town, but I thought I should go anyway. Even walking around the grocery store would be better than not doing anything.

So I drove to town and went grocery shopping. It was calming to walk through the aisles, putting things into my cart. But it wasn't until I was headed home and passing the Royal that I realized the real reason I'd been willing to get in the car. Before I could even really think about what I was doing, I slowed down and began to look for the truck. I didn't remember the license plate number, but it didn't matter: I was looking for a blue Ford with Wyoming plates.

I circled the block and even drove down some of the side streets, but the cowboy wasn't there. For a second I thought about going into the Royal to see with my own eyes that he wasn't there, but I didn't want to walk in the place. I was lonely, but there was nothing to do for it—at least I knew that. So I told myself, *Just go home. Just go home and call Julian.*

But it was not that simple. You could not have the amount of wanting I had inside me and be out in the world and not have the world send you something back. Or so it seemed to me, because when I pulled up to the cabin, I saw that someone had been there while I was gone. Not because of a garage door left ajar and or a note quickly penned—I knew it because someone had left a half-empty beer bottle on the stoop of the cabin, tucked beside the door.

3 5

HE, HIM, GABRIEL—though I never called him by his full name—came to the cabin around midnight. I was waiting.

"You didn't even wait until the bar closed this time," I said. "I'm flattered."

"Jesus Christ, I was here earlier. You were the one who wasn't here."

"Did you ever think of calling? Do you ever just call people?"

"I'm here now."

"I know," I said. "I saw the bottle. I looked for you in town."

"Why? Why would you look for me there?"

"Because I can feel you out there," I said. "Don't you get it? I can feel you out there somewhere."

"I'm in between places. Can we leave it at that?"

This time I was the one who took a step toward him. I rubbed my fingertips and then my hand over the fly of his jeans and over his cock.

"What places are you between?" I said. "Here and Blackduck? Here and Thief River?"

All I got for an answer were his hands on my breasts and between my legs. We were done talking for the time.

A little later, though, after we'd made it into the bedroom and were stripping down, he saw my bare patch of skin and said, "Jesus Christ, what did you do?"

I didn't answer. I knew what he was thinking: he wondered if he was the only one I was fucking. But there was no answer for that. I wasn't fucking anyone else, but I would never tell the cowboy about Breville. It was none of his business anyway.

"Do you like it?" I said.

For an answer the cowboy shook his head and kept looking at me. I still didn't explain anything. Let him go on looking.

When we got on the bed, he made me lie back and spread my legs wide. He ran his fingers over the skin.

"It's like you want to play or something," he said, and his voice sounded far away and a little angry—not so different from Breville's on the telephone.

"Do you like it?" I said again, but this time I had my palm around the base of his cock.

"What do you think?"

"Do you want to play with me?" I said.

"What do you think?"

I couldn't get anything else out of him, but when we were fucking, he kept saying, "I want to see it, I want to see it." So even though it was still easier for him to stand beside the bed and fuck me as I knelt, I kept having to turn over so he could look at my cunt. He wanted to get so far inside me with his hands and his face and his cock that it seemed like there wasn't enough of my body. As for me, the thing I wanted most was his mouth. When we kissed I rubbed my tongue hard over his teeth so I could feel their edges, and I kept my fingers by our lips so I could feel us kiss. I bit his lips and I sucked his tongue and I drank his spit. And no matter how we fucked or where he came, the cowboy howled. But no matter how much the cowboy howled, he never did get to the end of me.

Sometime in the night I got up from the bed and went down to the dock to swim, and again he didn't stir, just as he hadn't the first time we were together. But when I got back into bed, he reached over to the back of my neck and wrapped his hand with my wet hair.

"Do you have to go and wash it away?" he said in the darkness.

"It's not that."

"What is it, then?"

"It cools me," I said.

He didn't say anything else, but I got the feeling he wasn't asleep. I kept myself awake, listening to his breathing, to the way he moved on the bed, but then I must have fallen asleep, too, because the next time I opened my eyes the room was blue and I knew I'd had some kind of dream and his hand wasn't in my hair anymore.

This time when the cowboy was leaving, he didn't say, *I'll call you in a couple days*, or *I'll see you soon*, or *We'll make some plans*—we were done with the pretense. Instead we just lay down on the bed and he sucked my pussy one last time. Then he was gone.

3 6

THE NEXT DAY WAS MONDAY and I was supposed to be driving down to Stillwater, but when I woke up, I didn't want to go. Even though I spent most of Sunday napping after the cowboy left, my head was tired and I felt achy—from not enough sleep, I knew, but also from everything that had gone on in the last few days. I was on overload, and it reminded me a little of the mixed-up way I used to feel when I was in my teens and early twenties and always seemed to be teetering on the edge of one crisis or another. It had taken me a long time to understand most people didn't live like that, with constant drama in their lives, and I wondered at myself now. It seemed clear I was doing the same old thing all over again with Breville and the cowboy.

There was a quieter way to live, I knew—it was why I'd come north and it was what I pursued half the time. It was why I went on long swims, why I spent afternoons reading and napping on the dock, why I bought a red Huffy three-speed bike with coaster brakes at the Ace Hardware in town. I didn't think you could still get a bike with coaster brakes, and now I had one. I even bought one of those tacky plastic baskets with flowers on it for the handlebars, and the whole thing made me happy. But dozens of things had made me happy this summer: the painted turtle that floated into me one day, listening to Merle tell me his recipe for boiling up the jewelweed that grew along the lakeshore to make a tincture for poison ivy, or the way everyone in one town diner reminded me of a Thoreau essay from 1860 that talked about "men who are not above their business, whose coats are not too black, whose shoes do not shine very much." They were small things—some of them just moments—but they were real, and I trusted them, so much that I'd staked the next year of my life on them. Because even though I said I was taking the new job because I wanted a change, it mattered to me what kind of change it was. If I didn't think I could make a different kind of life up here for myself, and a better one somehow, I never would have accepted the offer.

But along with believing in smaller bits of happiness, I also believed in my own strong emotions, and the way I felt when I was in the thick of something vivid. And that was how I felt now. Whatever and whoever Breville and the cowboy were, my experiences with them were real. What I felt was real, and I could not walk away from the intensity of my feelings for either of them, no matter how unwise my emotions were. And I could not walk away from feeling itself.

But on this particular day I'd had enough. I wanted the day to myself. I knew Breville was waiting to see me down in Stillwater, but after fretting about it for a moment, I decided it would be good for him to wait a day to see me. Not because I wanted to punish him for his reaction to me on the phone the other night, and not because I wanted to pay him back for the wasted trip I'd made when he was on lockdown. Rather, I thought it would be good for him to wait a day to see me because he was the one who told me I did not need to do his time with him. On this particular day my life—my real life, not the artificial one I shared with him in the visiting room at Stillwater—had intervened. I was tired from fucking the cowboy. I didn't want to drive four hours to the Cities. That was all.

I didn't owe anyone anything, I told myself. Not the cowboy and not Breville. Especially not Breville.

After I napped most of the afternoon on the dock, I rode my bike partway around the lake. I went past the place Merle called "the scar," which was a steep lake lot where the owners had cut away all the trees between their house and the lake so they could have a view and a big sand beach. If Merle was really riled up, he called it "the goddamn scar upon the land" and couldn't stop cursing.

"They took out every living thing," Merle said when he explained the history of the place to me. "Except that all those trees and all the brush they chopped out were holding the slope in place. Now it's falling into the lake. Goddamn fools."

Even though I never saw the lot before the trees had been cut, it was plain enough why Merle was upset. The house itself was large and gleaming white, and with its trucked-in sand and lack of vegetation, the entire place stood out from the rest of the heavily treed lakeshore. But that was the way it was done up here sometimes. I often spotted lots and tracts that had been logged, and they were almost always clear-cut, with nothing left but broken trunks and slash. Garbage.

I didn't know what made the next idea come into my mind, but standing there with one foot down on the ground and the other still on the pedal of my bike, I thought, that's what a rape was like. A clear-cut. All experiences removed except the rape. It seemed like a powerful image, and for a moment I stood there, thinking about it.

Then I rejected it.

A woman's body, my body, wasn't a forest, and whatever damage

I experienced as a result of my rape was exactly that: pain from an act of violence that had nothing to do with me. Someone fucked me and bit me until he tore my skin, and I didn't want to use any other words for it. Whatever else my life was, it was not a clear-cut.

I thought about that as I pedaled away from the scar, but in a little while the thought itself dissipated in the tiny breeze I made as I rode, there beside the lake.

37

THE NEXT DAY was windy and rainy, only in the fifties, and I shivered the three blocks from the parking lot to the door of Stillwater prison. I'd stopped at the rest area in Rogers on the way into the Cities to fix my hair and take off my panties, and now I was wearing just a fancy corset with garters and no crotch. The thing had stiff ribbing in it to hold my breasts up and out, and all the way down the street I was hoping the ribbing was plastic so I didn't set off the metal detector with underwires.

But I didn't set off the detector, and just like every other time, after they announced "Visit for Breville," I got to pass into the small, locked holding cell, and through the second locking door, and into the visiting room and toward Breville. When we embraced in the taped-off square, he quickly ran his hands down my sides, but I didn't know if he could feel the end of the corset or not.

"You smell good, as always," he said into my hair, and then we were pulling apart.

The room had a few people in it, just the way Breville promised it would—enough people for the guards to monitor but not so many as to make us feel crowded. As I sat down, I used the motion of arranging my dress to slip open another button.

"So, tell me about this new job," Breville said as he watched my fingers. "Why do you need a change?"

"I don't want to be in the Cities anymore," I said. "I want to do something different."

"Aren't you going to miss things?"

"I don't think so. I haven't missed anything this summer."

"You know I can't call you up there. I can't pay for it."

"You can call me collect."

"I don't like that. I never have. It makes me feel bad not to be able to pay for my calls."

"I'll visit. At least on the weekends. We'll talk then. I need to be up there," I said.

As I said that, he opened his legs and then brought them together again and began to bounce one leg up and down. I doubted that either one of us had paid any attention to the things we'd just said—the real thing going on between us, and the only thing, was there between Breville's legs and mine. The words we said were just noise.

"Are you nervous?" I said, and looked at his bouncing leg.

"Just waiting. Anticipation."

I knew it was my cue, but something in me felt scared: not so much of showing Breville my little-girl bareness, but of being caught.

But I did it. I opened my legs. Breville slouched down in his chair and looked, and I opened my legs even farther when he leaned down to retie his shoelace. He looked at me a long time, and then returned to slouching. In a little while he bent down to retie the other shoe.

He studied my vulva the way I had studied his face the first time I came to see him.

When he sat back up, he looked down at his lap and then at my eyes and then back down at his cock. I looked at his jeans and I could see the mounded fabric. His erection wasn't obvious—it could have just been the denim and the way he was sitting—but he looked thick. Swollen. When I looked back at his face to meet his eyes, though, he had turned away. When he turned back to face me, he looked upset.

"Are you happy?" I said. "To see me today?"

"Of course I am."

"You don't seem happy."

"I'm happy."

"Okay. I guess I'll believe you."

"I don't know. What do you want me to say? It depresses me."

"What does?"

"You know. It just depresses me to see it."

It took me a few seconds, but then I understood. I understood what he had just said, and I drew my legs together. Not that he saw—he was still looking away from me. Looking around the visiting room to see who else was there, who he could flash a hand sign to, looking for Gates. I didn't know.

But that was the power men and boys had. They could say your vagina smelled and made their fingers stink, or that good pussy didn't just lie there. They could say your cunt depressed them.

We sat silently for a while and then Breville said, "Is it pierced?"

When I shook my head no, he said, "I thought I saw metal."

"Maybe it was a garter."

"Well, at least you can tell it's shaved," he said. "Did you ever think about getting it pierced?"

"No. I never thought about it."

"Maybe you'd like it. It would probably be exciting."

"Maybe," I said, but it didn't matter. He was hardly looking at me. I'd served it up to him on a platter, and he'd already lost interest.

Yet what exactly did I expect? Breville might have stopped

drinking in prison and he might have been prevented from hurting anyone else, but on some level he was still the same damaged person he'd been when he raped. He didn't get healthier in prison. He didn't want to lose himself in the animal wetness of my body. He wanted to shave it and pierce it. Puncture and slice it.

We talked awhile longer, but I couldn't make myself stay the two hours we were allotted. After some desultory story Breville managed to come up with, I told him I needed to head out. Back to the cabin. Back home.

"They're predicting storms," I said.

"I haven't seen lightning in seven years," he told me. "Never thought I'd miss it, but I do."

"It's still the same," I said. "It still lights up the sky."

"I even miss snow," Breville said. "What do you think of that? I wouldn't even mind shoveling some, you know?"

It was a repeat of something he'd written in a letter. I smiled at him but didn't say anything, and then we stood up to walk over to the taped-off square.

For the last time, I said goodbye to Breville in front of the guard. He passed his hand over my hip and ass but this time I didn't feel any burning. Just the touch of his hand. What had I wanted from him, really? And I thought, if I couldn't count on sexual interest from a rapist, then who?

Bare-pussied and cold, I wondered that the whole way home.

3 8

WHEN I GOT HOME to the cabin, the worst of the wind had died down, so I went for a swim. There was nothing else to do.

The water was warmer than the air, so once I was in, it felt like any other summer day. I swam a hundred feet out and then started going back and forth, back and forth. I didn't have words for the lowness I felt. I felt ridiculous. Was ridiculous.

I wondered if Frank L—— even knew he'd raped me. It probably just seemed like a fuck to him. He'd been stoned, drinking. Even though I cried, I didn't know if it really registered with him. And even though he asked me once if my cunt hurt, my answer meant nothing to him, because he went on fucking me. And I fucked him back, at least for a time. And even if he was aware of what he did that night, I was sure he didn't think of me the way I thought of him—weekly, maybe almost daily—for the past seventeen years. What faithfulness I had to him. But I doubted he remembered my name.

As I swam, I thought about the other thing I never told anyone about my rape. I always thought I kept it a secret because I was ashamed of my actions. I was, but I also didn't tell anyone because I figured no one would ever believe or understand what I did.

One day, about a month after I was raped, I still felt low and flat and blank. The day was cool and gray, and all I wanted to do was sleep. Every time I felt myself drifting into sleep and entering the shell of a dream, though, the neighbor's dog began to bark. The barking brought me back to the gray day and my cold room. The dog woke me three times, and after the third time, I knew I wouldn't be able to sleep the day away. I didn't know what to do instead, but then something in me did know, and I took off the pale blue nightgown I was sleeping in and I got dressed.

He was often at Ty Kintzel's house—or so I judged because I knew his truck and often saw it parked there by the canal. The entire town was a corral where people were penned.

When Ty Kintzel opened the door, I nodded at him.

"He here?"

Kintzel didn't answer but motioned me in and pulled the door closed behind me. The hallway was dark and we walked back to the living room.

Kintzel had to say Keil's name to get him to look up from the television, which was blaring. The place reeked, so I knew the two of them had been sitting there and smoking and smoking. Some game was on. Keil looked up when he heard Ty, and that was the only time he looked at me. It was the first time I'd seen him since he held me for Frank, and it wasn't until I saw his face that I really knew what I had come for. I thought if I could say I wanted a piece of what had happened, or if I could say I'd wanted Keil and wanted him still, it would make the other night something I controlled.

Keil Ward looked at me for a moment, and then he told Ty, "I already been there. I guess it's your turn." Then he went back to watching TV.

Kintzel looked at me and I looked back. He was all right: over six feet tall, brown hair. A little gone to fat. I knew he went with a girl who had been a couple years ahead of me in school. Yvette Cameron.

Kintzel said, "Sit down."

So I did. The three of us passed a joint for a while. Or rather, Kintzel passed it to me and took it back from me, then passed it over to Keil. After a while, Ty Kintzel said to me, "Do you want to see the rest of the house?" and I knew he had decided.

When we got to the bedroom, I guess he still thought he had to talk me into something. He said to me, "That shirt you got on—it gets me excited."

I pulled it off. Then I took off my bra so he could see my breasts, envy of Cheryl Korr.

We didn't talk after that.

When Kintzel put his face between my legs, I let him. I was all done with my medication, and the tiny tears in my skin had healed. After a little while I pulled at Kintzel's shoulders until he moved up over me and got inside. I kept looking at the wallpaper in the room, at the dark furniture, which looked like it came from someone's grandmother. I put my hands on Kintzel's back for a second, and then took them away. It was a gentle fuck. I hardly felt his dick moving into me.

The whole thing took a few minutes. Right before the end, Kintzel gave me a few extra strokes.

"That's for you," he said.

After he rolled off me, I stuck my hands down between my legs and, sure enough, I found that slipperiness. I hadn't felt him come.

I was dressed before Kintzel. When I opened the bedroom door, he was still sitting there on the bed, tying his laces.

"I had a good time," he said. "Thanks."

"I had a good time, too," I said.

Before I walked out of that house, I looked once more at Keil

Ward, at the side of his face as he sat watching TV. He didn't seem like the person who had flirted with me all those months, and he didn't seem like the person who had watched as someone else fucked me. He didn't seem like anyone. I had come to Keil Ward again because I'd wanted something from him, wanted to settle something from that night, and it was just my luck that he didn't want to fuck me. Just my luck. But I didn't let myself think about that. I kept moving to the door.

When I got outside, my eyes felt like they were far back in my head and I knew I was miles away from my body. Ty Kintzel's come had canceled out Frank L——'s. I'd thought I needed Keil Ward, since he had been there that night, but as it turned out, what Kintzel had done was empty enough for me. It got the job done.

I never told anyone about what I'd done the day I went looking for Keil Ward because I didn't think they would understand how it brought things back to nil. But it made perfect sense to me then, and it made perfect sense to me still. I didn't get stuck in my rape. Or maybe I did get stuck, but not in the same way I would have if I hadn't kept touching people, or letting them touch me. If I hadn't kept spreading my legs.

But maybe if I had told people how I hunted down Keil Ward— or how, when he turned me away, I found a substitute quarry and replacement cock—it would have helped them understand what kind of person I was. Maybe it would have kept them from seeing me as a victim. For instance, when Richaux and I used to be fucking or getting ready to fuck, he sometimes told me he could feel scars. "They make me think of that other night," he'd tell me, even when I hadn't been thinking of it at all, when I'd been enjoying his fingers or his cock inside me.

He wasn't the only one who said things like that, either—learning about my rape just seemed to immobilize some men. I guess I didn't blame them. But hearing a man's response was a torturous thing in itself, and I often didn't tell men at all. If I felt I had to explain some of my strangeness about not being able to sleep beside them, or the weird, visceral response I had when I smelled someone's unwashed hair, I just said it was one of my idiosyncrasies.

And yet, what did I expect from men, really, when I myself had such confused feelings about the rape? Sometimes I felt like the rape had marred me and shaped me, and other times I felt like I was exactly who I was meant to be. In any case, the experience was mine, and it was mine to deal with as I could.

After I swam, I came back to the cabin. Made myself eggs and toast. After I ate, I climbed into bed. Let myself stop thinking. Let myself sleep.

39

THERE WAS A COOL STILLNESS TO THE LAKE in September. I could feel the quietness as I swam and floated, and it seemed to go many feet down. Certainly fewer boats churned the lake, forcing wave after wave against the shoreline, but it wasn't just that. The water itself felt heavier on my hands—the difference between silk and velvet. I swam every day after I came home from school, and by the time I got in the water, the sun was usually low on the horizon. As the month went on and I kept at it, Merle told me I was crazy. Yet even if I'd tried, I don't think I could have explained how I liked the deep quiet I felt in the water, or how swimming slowly helped me put the day behind me.

On this particular afternoon I was thinking of a student who had such difficulty reading that, at fifteen, she was still puzzling over *was* and *saw*. I knew from her records that she was special ed and dyslexic, but today I'd handed back a paper in which she'd written *I was a bird* instead of *I saw a bird*, and I could not stop thinking of the beauty of that particular error. One sentence observation, the other being and experience.

"I think you may be a poet, Cher," I told her when I gave her the sheet of notebook paper. She smiled, and it was the first time I'd seen her do that since classes began.

With the start of school and the rush to shape lessons and learn names, it was easy enough to push away thoughts of Breville. But of course I did think of him. In the days after that last visit, he hadn't tried to call, but a couple weeks later, a slender letter finally arrived. I waited a day before I read it. When I did, I went as far as the sentence that said, *I think I am now ready for a relationship with you,* and then I stopped. I didn't know if Breville was asking for something or telling me what he had to offer, but it didn't matter. Whatever his definition of good pussy was, I didn't want to meet it. I didn't need his particular brand of sickness in my life.

I hadn't seen the cowboy since the night he left the beer bottle by my door. But if he was persistent, as able to sniff me out as he seemed to be, he'd have no trouble finding me once I moved to Merle's. Or maybe I'd never see him again. I didn't have a phone number for him except for the one in Blackduck, didn't even know how to spell his last name. I wasn't sure we'd know what to do with each other when we weren't inside each other's bodies. And as much as I craved him, his destitution scared me. Of all the things about him to be scared by, I thought it was telling that I chose his lack of money. But at least something about him scared me.

When I got out of the water, I pushed myself up onto the dock, going from weightlessness to gravity. But instead of hurrying back to the cabin and dry clothes, I decided to stand still. There beside the dock, dripping lake water, I stood motionless for five, fifteen, thirty minutes.

No boats went by and no car came down the gravel road.

Birds resumed their flight.

A heron came to land on the bank not twenty feet away.

A muskrat swam out from the shoreline, making a V-shaped wake.

I stood so long that my skin began to warm, and my blood heated the water that kept dripping from me.

When I made my way back to the yellow light I'd left burning in the cabin, it was already going dark. But the furnace of my heart kept me warm, and I passed through the air like air.

ACKNOWLEDGMENTS

Thank you to: Nicole Aragi, who is beyond compare; the Bush Foundation, which gave me a Bush Artist Fellowship that helped change my life; the Mill Foundation and Santa Fe Art Institute, for a crucial writing residency.

CPSIA information can be obtained at www.ICGtesting.com
Printed in the USA
LVOW062210210513

334936LV00004B/50/P